LOVE,

Secret
Santa

LOVE,
Secret Santa

S.A. DOMINGO

Hodder
Children's
Books

HODDER CHILDREN'S BOOKS

First published in Great Britain in 2019 by Hodder and Stoughton

1 3 5 7 9 10 8 6 4 2

Text copyright © Hodder & Stoughton Ltd, 2019

*All characters and events in this publication, other than those clearly
in the public domain, are fictitious and any resemblance to
real persons, living or dead, is purely coincidental.*

A CIP catalogue record for this book
is available from the British Library.

ISBN 978 1 44495 375 6

Printed and bound in Great Britain
by Clays Ltd, Elcograf S.p.A.

The paper and board used in this book
are made from wood from responsible sources

MIX
Paper from
responsible sources
FSC® C104740

Hodder Children's Books
An imprint of
Hachette Children's Group
Part of Hodder and Stoughton
Carmelite House
50 Victoria Embankment
London EC4Y 0DZ

An Hachette UK Company
www.hachette.co.uk

www.hachettechildrens.co.uk

To Will, Valda, Larry and Lawrence,
and all my friends, for their unwavering
support. And to the young women who
deserve to see themselves in stories.

CHAPTER 1

Sunday 30th November

Fat, soft flakes of snow swirled down towards the concourse below as Angel Green gazed out of the café window. *Finally.* It really was starting to feel like Christmas was around the corner, even if she had so much to cram in between now and the end of term. The town's ice rink was being assembled in the open square, like it was every year, and Angel felt a buzz of anticipation as she watched the people in their high-visibility vests setting it up. Christmas songs had just begun to intersperse the terrible chart music being pumped out from the speakers in the café, and Angel wasn't even annoyed by them. Not yet anyway! The whole thing was so mesmerising, she almost forgot the chemistry textbook open on the table in front of her, and her rapidly cooling hot chocolate.

'Gorgeous,' she whispered absently as she observed the scene, her breath clouding against the cool glass.

'I know, right?'

Angel turned towards her best friend, Izzy Carter – but the brunette was scrunching her curls to reinvigorate their signature perky bounce, her keen blue eyes trained in an entirely different direction. Craning her head to see between the busy tables towards where Izzy was looking, Angel could make out a vaguely familiar figure in a black leather jacket. He had a tan scarf wound around his neck despite being indoors, but Angel had to admit she was impressed at how well it complemented his light-brown skin and perfectly styled dark quiff. Sanj Patel *was* gorgeous. But Angel frowned in confusion at Izzy's preening. Sanj had only joined their school in the summer, but he'd almost instantly begun – and then ended – a passionate affair with Henry Reeves.

'Err, I don't think Sanj is—' Angel began, but then her gaze settled on the *true* object of Izzy's affection as her friend breathed: '*Manny. Patel. Like, how is he even more delicious every time I see him?*'

Ah. Sanj's older brother, Manav. Equally gorgeous, two years older than them. Angel knew her friend's hopes of attracting *his* attention were minimal at best, but in the spirit of impending Christmas good cheer, she didn't want to burst her bubble. Izzy practically drooled watching Manny nonchalantly lick some whipped cream off his finger. He handed his brother the sports section of the Sunday newspaper they seemed to be sharing, and they both laughed about something. Angel sighed – sometimes she wished she had a sibling to hang out with like that. Then again, Izzy was practically a sister to her, even if a slightly delusional one.

'Reel it in, Izz,' she said with a laugh, and her friend finally turned back to their table. Angel smoothed over the page of the textbook she'd been studying and picked her highlighter pen back up.

'*You* reel it in,' Izzy retorted, reaching over to fish out a mini marshmallow from Angel's drink. 'The weekend is practically over. You can let go of the studying for one measly afternoon, Ange.'

'You can hang out with Ola.'

'No, I can't. Ola's busy rehearsing for some drama club end of term production and—'

'Oi!'

Angel and Izzy both turned as Karl, the usually almost-too-relaxed owner of the Crafty Cuppa café, went over to the corner table to admonish the rowdy group of boys getting a bit overenthusiastic about the YouTube videos they were watching on someone's phone.

'Sorry, Karl. Sorry, mate,' one of them said with a chuckle. His deep, irritatingly familiar voice caused Angel to roll her eyes. *Caspar Johnson.* One of the most popular boys in their school, and one of the most annoyingly arrogant. Ugh. Angel felt her festive mood starting to wane.

'I have to study, Izzy,' she said, turning back to her friend. 'You know there's no way I'm going to get into Dunstable Academy without that scholarship. And they've got the best—'

'A-level science departments in the country, yeah, yeah, I know,' Izzy finished, with an affectionate smile. 'I also know that there's no way you're not going to be *Doctor* Angel Green within a few years, Dunstable Academy or no. Don't put so much pressure on yourself! We're sixteen. We're meant to be having some fun!'

'Fun is a myth to me until that scholarship exam on the twentieth,' Angel replied, taking a mouthful of no-longer-hot chocolate with a grimace. She nudged her mobile phone as it rested on the table. The screen lit up with the familiar background image of Angel and her mother, Ruth, grinning with their cheeks pressed together. Identical glowing, deep-brown skin, sculpted lips and wide, dark eyes ... Angel smiled back at the image – then noticed the time.

'Hang on, it's nearly five o'clock already?' She started gathering up her textbooks and pens, shoving them into her backpack. 'I said I'd meet Mum and help her carry the shopping home after her shift.'

Izzy nodded, pulling a thick, well-worn novel from her backpack. Beauty tutorial videos and books were her twin passions. Angel loved that her friend wasn't easy to pin down. 'I think I'm going to chill here for a bit,' Izzy said, her eyes drifting back over to the Patel brothers' table. 'You know, enjoy the view . . .'

Angel laughed, pulling on her mustard-yellow coat and winding her fluffy green scarf around her neck. She swung her bag on to her shoulder and bent down to kiss Izzy's cheek quickly. 'If you say so. Be good!'

She made her way between the buzzing tables in the café and headed outside, aiming for the stairs down to the concourse. But as she hurried around the corner outside the Crafty Cuppa, she smacked headlong into a solid chest, and felt two strong hands grip her shoulders to steady her.

'Thank—' She cut herself off as she pushed her long box braids out of her eyes – eyes which travelled up to meet those of the stranger who'd prevented her collapse. They were hazel; crinkled in mirth at the corners, and set in a supposedly handsome face. 'Oh.' Not a stranger after all.

Caspar Johnson grinned his typical, irritating grin down at her. 'You're welcome,' he said cockily, letting go of her to bend down and pick up his wallet from the ground, where it had fallen during their collision. He dusted it off pointedly. 'Karl's new cash-only policy means some pretty tedious trips to the cash point, right?'

Angel fought the urge to roll her eyes again. She wasn't looking for an explanation as to what Caspar was up to, and she also wasn't looking to chat. 'Mmm,' she said noncommittally, moving to edge past him. 'I'm actually late to meet my mum, so—'

Caspar's expression softened. 'Oh, right, cool. Say hi to Ruth for me.'

Angel pursed her lips, but she had to admit it was sort of nice, if a bit weird, that Caspar still thought fondly of her mum. She and Caspar's parents had spent lots of time together, back when they were little. Caspar's dad, Oscar, had been really good friends with Angel's father. Her shoulders sagged a bit, as memories she could have done without flooded her mind suddenly: being at Caspar's as their families barbequed on a summer's day, having water fights with Caspar, her mother laughing as she told them off half-heartedly.

She and Caspar had been really good friends once. Of course, that was a long time ago, before her dad had died and their families drifted apart, and *long* before they had got to secondary school, where Caspar had started to get 'popular' and act like she didn't exist . . . Since then, the only time he'd paid her any attention was that one day she'd let him copy her history homework, because he seemed so desperate – and that had almost landed her in the only real trouble she'd ever been in at school. Angel shuddered, remembering how it was sheer luck that a fire drill had distracted Ms Evans from catching them. Caspar had made no attempt to apologise, and Angel had never really got over that. He knew how important school was for her.

Forget all of that, she told herself. It was years ago now, she'd moved on. Caspar certainly had. It was just annoying that he was permanently so *smug*. Caspar Johnson always got away with things, coasting through life, charming adults and their classmates alike to get out of trouble (or into it). And, of course, he was the object of affection for practically everyone with the potential to be interested at their school. Angel, on the other hand, felt like *she* had to fight for everything she got. She wasn't a *total* no-hoper, but she wasn't exactly the Kim K of her peers. Certainly not when it came to things like boys – or anyone else – checking her out . . .

'That's a pretty big backpack you've got there,' she tuned back in to hear Caspar saying, folding his arms. 'Might be throwing off your centre of balance, eh?' He crinkled his eyes at her.

'Some of us actually have to revise, Caspar, not just rely on how good we are at throwing ourselves around on a field or whatever.'

Caspar ran a hand over his soft brown afro now, and Angel was annoyed by the burst of familiarity at watching the curls spring back into place. He had used to do the same gesture when they were kids. She felt just a tiny bit bad at what she'd said, until he grinned smugly at her again.

'AG, d'you know what you *really* need to learn to do? *Relax*.'

Angel began to wonder how many times you could roll your eyes before they fell out of their sockets. 'Bye, Caspar.' She made to move past him, and he did a silly left-right shuffle as though there was no predicting which way she'd go, before finally stepping aside.

'See you at school,' he called over his shoulder as he headed back into the café.

'Yeah, right,' she mumbled.

Angel hurried away towards the Bluebell Hospice, huddling against the cold evening air.

Her mum's work was only a five-minute walk away, but she was grateful by the time she stepped into the warmth of the hospice's lobby. Seeing her mum talking to one of the other nurses behind the dilapidated reception desk in the lobby, Angel waved hello and then headed over to one of the orange plastic chairs in the waiting area, sighing as she sat down.

The staff had obviously started to do some Christmas decorating in anticipation of the start of December, but the tinsel looked a bit sparse and sad, especially as it hung in droops along the faded yellow walls. Angel had never really thought about how shabby the hospice was – it must be pretty depressing for the patients coming there, and for their families. Angel knew that people came to the hospice when they were really quite ill and needed special care. If she had time, she thought, she might volunteer to help spruce things up a bit there. But between school and her scholarship studies, Angel felt like she barely had a moment to think right now, let alone help anyone else . . .

'Hiya, sweetheart,' her mum said, heading towards Angel at last, with her coat on over her pale blue nurse's uniform. 'Ready?'

'Yeah,' Angel said, standing and hoisting her – admittedly rather heavy – backpack on to her shoulders again, while flipping her braids out of the way over her shoulder. Her mum reached over to hug her, chuckling.

'I know you paid good money for those things, but you really ought to tie them back, darling,' she said, gesturing to her daughter's hair. 'All this falling in front of your face can't be very convenient.'

Angel smiled wryly, thinking how she'd had to save up to get her hair braided. OK, maybe they were a bit long and '*impractical*' as her mum had been at pains to point out, but they looked *really* good. 'I manage fine,' she said, only half-truthfully.

They waved goodbye to the staff taking over for the night shift, and Angel looked at her mum as they made their way out of the squeaky sliding doors into the cold. Dark circles nestled under the older woman's eyes, and her footsteps seemed a bit heavy. Working at the hospice was draining stuff, Angel knew.

'Everything all right, Mum?' she asked as they headed towards the supermarket through the light dusting of snow. Ruth pulled one hand out of her pocket and reached over to squeeze Angel's briefly as they walked along.

'Fine, Ange. Just quite a sad day, that's all. One of our older patients might be quite near the end. It's tough for the family, you know, especially getting so close to Christmas and all.'

Angel nodded, squeezing back. She knew her mum couldn't really give too much detail about the patients at the hospice, or their families – they had to keep that kind of thing confidential. But she could only imagine how hard it must be on their loved ones.

'Hey, I know what might lift the mood,' Angel said, smiling over at her mum and stopping short outside the supermarket. 'We can get some bits and pieces for the week, but why don't we forget cooking tonight and get ourselves a Chinese takeaway? I've still got a bit of cash left over from the birthday card Grandma Joyce sent me.' Her dad's mum lived in Ghana, but she video called whenever she could, and was always generous with her gifts on special occasions. It was nice to have that connection to him. Angel tried to ignore the fact that this was the second time in half an hour she'd had a memory of her dad, but it was getting close to his birthday, which was always tough. She took a breath and looked at her mum, who seemed unsure.

'I don't want you to waste your money, sweetheart . . .'

But Angel's mind was made up. She could already taste the Sichuan chicken. 'I want to, Mum. You deserve it. And I *definitely* do. Come on, let's whip round the shop, and I'll ring Canton Kitchen when we're on the way home.'

Her mum grinned. 'I wouldn't say no to a spring roll or two.'

'Or three,' Angel said, nudging her mum with her shoulder.

An hour or so later, Angel and her mum finally sat back from their little kitchen table with matching, satisfied sighs.

'That was delicious. Thanks, darling. I feel much better!' her mum said, standing to start clearing away the empty foil containers and their plates. She turned towards the sink, but as she did, Angel noticed her mum's phone screen light up with a message, followed by a ping announcing its arrival. She didn't mean to pry, but her brows knit together in curiosity as she saw an unfamiliar name above the notification – Victor? Angel was even more suspicious when her mum quickly turned back to the table and picked up her phone, smiling at the message as she opened it. She'd seen that look before – on Izzy's love-struck face when she'd found the next object of her affection. Could her mum be *dating* someone?

Angel wasn't quite sure how to feel about that. Since her father died it had just been the two of them. Her mum had pretty much never dated anyone before that Angel knew about, anyway, and she wasn't sure she wanted to ask about it. She pulled a face at the thought of her mum fancying someone at all, and then hoped she hadn't noticed. Maybe it *might* be a good thing for her mum to have something nice to look forward to. At least one of them might have some sort of a love life!

Ew. Angel wrinkled up her nose again, and quickly started clearing the rest of the table.

'Right,' Angel announced after she had finished, and her mum looked up from over the rim of her glasses, which she had put on to type out her reply on her phone, painfully slowly. 'I'm going to do a bit more studying before bed. Night, Mum!'

'Night, Ange,' her mother replied distractedly, turning back to her phone. It felt like some kind of weird role reversal for her mum to be eagerly texting a boy – *man* – and Angel to be going off to bed! 'Oh, darling?'

Angel paused at the bottom of the stairs, and looked back over. 'Yeah?'

'Thank you for dinner.' She looked a bit sad again.

Angel took the couple of strides across their tiny living space to give her mum a kiss on the cheek. 'No worries, Mum.'

'Listen, I know things have been a bit tight lately, you know, money-wise.' Angel felt her face go serious as her mum continued. 'I want you to do well at this exam, because I know how much that school means to you. I really wish I could afford it without the scholarship, but—'

'Mum, it's fine—'

Ruth shook her head. 'But,' she said a bit louder, in her 'overruled' voice, 'I know *wherever* you go, you're going to be a superstar. Know why?' She grinned suddenly at Angel. 'Because you were raised by one!'

Angel laughed. 'Night, Mum,' she said again.

As she settled on to her bed with her lamp concentrated over the books spread out around her, Angel decided to reach over and open the curtains. She felt that warm, Christmassy feeling all over again as she saw more snowflakes tumbling down from the dark night sky. Maybe she *did* need to take some time out to . . .

Relax?

For some reason, she heard Caspar's voice in her head, of all people. God, why was she thinking about what stupid Caspar Johnson said to her? Shaking her head, she took one last look at the swirling snow before turning back to her books.

CHAPTER 2

Monday 1st December

Angel's eyes drifted open. Something wide and flat was pressing down on her face. She felt around with her hands until her fingers connected with the smooth cover of . . . a textbook. She'd fallen asleep studying! Peeling the pages from her cheek, Angel sat up and felt around desperately for her mobile phone to check the time.

'Nooo!' Twenty minutes until school started – and her school was a *ten-minute* walk away. Why hadn't her mum woken her up? Then Angel remembered that she worked the early shift on Mondays, so she would have left for the hospice at six o'clock in the morning. Normally Angel would have set her alarm but obviously—

No time for regrets. She leapt out of her bed, whipping off the silk bonnet she slept in to keep her hair neat, and crammed the scattered books into her backpack in preparation for grabbing it the minute she was ready. Running to the bathroom, she showered and brushed her teeth at the same time, dried off so quickly that the friction could have started a campfire, slathered some lotion on – she wasn't willing to be ashy, regardless of how late she was running – and threw on her school uniform, including the crinkled shirt she'd totally forgotten to iron the night before. Sparing ten seconds to look in the mirror, she smiled because at least her braids still looked great.

No time for vanity, though! Grabbing her coat, scarf and backpack, Angel legged it out of the house and broke the land-speed record for a teenage girl rushing along the high street, texting Izzy as she went to tell her she was running late so to head on to school without her. But even with her epic hustling, Angel had long missed the first bell. She saw Mrs Black tutting at the doors to the school and tapping her watch at the stragglers.

'Not like you, Ms Green,' the headteacher said – but then her eyes lifted towards someone behind Angel.

She heard rapid footsteps race up alongside her, and looked around to see . . . *Of course*. Caspar Johnson, tie loose and shirt barely tucked in, smiling as he looked between Angel and Mrs Black in a way that he clearly thought was charming.

'Morning, Mrs Black!' he said cheerfully. 'Hey, Angel.' Their headteacher pursed her lips.

'Late as usual, Mr Johnson. And might I suggest getting fully dressed before arriving at—'

Caspar was nodding, but before their headteacher could finish, he interjected with, 'I was *so* inspired by your assembly on Friday, by the way, Mrs B.' He looked at the older woman earnestly. 'So much food for thought about making sure we reduce congestion in the corridors.

Inspirational, to be honest. You've just got that gift with words, you know?'

Mrs Black genuinely looked flattered, and almost seemed to forget about Angel being late, or there at all, as she and Caspar strode together into the school. 'Why thank you, Mr Johnson. I try to keep you young people engaged, you know . . .'

Angel was midway through a classic eye-roll when she saw Caspar look over his shoulder from where he'd been nodding along to Mrs Black – and actually *wink* at her. *God,* he was arrogant! As he clutched the strap of his schoolbag, Angel noticed that his hands seemed to be covered in flecks of blue paint. Was that why he was late – because he'd been messing about with art stuff? In spite of herself, Angel found curiosity rising about what he might be making, but she quickly shook herself out of it.

'Now, aren't you two due at the school council meeting during first lesson?' Mrs Black asked. She seemed to finally remember that Angel had been trailing sheepishly behind them. 'We extend that privilege to council members because you are meant to be *responsible*,' she said, looking over her thin glasses frames at Angel as she emphasised the last word. Why was she – Miss Punctuality, usually – being singled out over the shambles that was Caspar Johnson? Angel was certain he was only on the school council to begin with because of the perks – and because he always managed to charm the teachers.

Angel sighed. 'Sorry, miss. Yes, I'm heading straight there.'

'Me too,' Caspar said, falling back a bit so that he could match strides with Angel now. As the headteacher turned away in the other direction towards her office, Caspar saluted her and then spun on his heel. 'Let's go, AG.'

'Stop calling me that.' Angel sighed once again, and followed as Caspar bustled in the direction of the classroom where they held the council meeting. She wondered if this Monday morning could possibly get any more *Mondaaay Moooorning* before the clock even struck 10 am.

'After you,' Caspar said, holding the door for Angel as they arrived. She glanced up at him, narrowing her eyes suspiciously at him seeming to be polite for once, but then headed inside.

'*Finally*,' came a high, piercing voice as the eight students assembled around a table in the centre of the room turned to look at Angel and Caspar arriving. Tilda Chase smoothed one hand over her sleek auburn ponytail, as though their lateness may have caused a hair to slip out of place. 'Take a seat please, guys, we don't have that long.'

Angel mumbled her apologies to the others and slipped into a seat next to Aiko Malcom, who smiled sympathetically. Caspar, of course, received an elaborate fist-bump of greeting from Josh Yorke, his best friend. They were seemingly oblivious to the steam beginning to gently leak from Tilda's ears. Angel pulled out her notebook as Olivia Wilson, Tilda's right-hand-woman, started handing out sheets of paper with 'AGENDA' printed boldly at the top. Given that there was only 'charity fundraiser' and a couple of other sentences written underneath it, Angel was pretty sure it was just so Tilda and Oliva felt official in their roles as chair and deputy chair of the council. Caspar caught her eye as she glanced up from the sheet of paper, and smiled like he could read her thoughts. She ignored him, and he picked up a pencil and began sketching an intricate design on the blank expanse of his own copy.

'Can we get started at last?' Tilda said now. 'As you should all know, today we are due to select our charity of choice for this year's Christmas fundraiser. Angel? Caspar?'

Angel startled, glancing over at Caspar again and then back over to Tilda. 'Uh, sorry?'

'You two were meant to be coming up with suggestions, as the charity sub-committee. Remember?'

Angel definitely didn't remember. It must have been buried in the minutes that Olivia sent round after the last meeting – she already had her laptop out now and was typing furiously. She liked to record every word, facial expression and sneeze that happened during the council meetings. Angel realised she must have been too distracted when the council last met. That was the day she'd found out she'd been invited to sit the scholarship exam for Dunstable Academy.

'Err . . .' Angel began, looking to Caspar for help, but he just shrugged. *Great.*

'Pigs!' Everyone turned to look at Adam Clarke, who was nodding enthusiastically. 'We should raise money for pigs! They get a bad rap, but really, they're just as clever as dogs. In fact, like my dad always says, cats look down at you, dogs look up to you . . . But pigs? Pigs look you right in the eye.' He pointed his index and pinkie fingers emphatically between his wide blue eyes and Tilda's horrified gaze.

'We are *not* "doing pigs",' Tilda grated out, and then sniffed. 'Besides, we supported a donkey sanctuary last year. Seriously, guys, we need to think of something. Angel?'

Angel's mind suddenly crystallised on the memory of the shabby walls and decorations at the hospice last night, and her mum's tired face. 'Wait, what about Bluebell Hospice?' she said enthusiastically. Out of the corner of her eye, she thought she saw Josh glance towards Caspar, who was now concentrating on his sketch with a degree of focus she'd never seen him put into anything. Probably trying to shirk his responsibility to this supposed sub-committee. Angel turned back to the rest of the council. 'They could really do with the money, and I know for a fact that they do some amazing work.'

'Let's put that to a vote, then,' Tilda said, nodding to Olivia, who spent several moments smoothing her blonde hair back behind her ears and pushing her glasses up her nose. Then she stood up and declared: 'I hereby open a vote on our charity of choice for Christmas this year.' She paused and bent down to type out what she'd said on her laptop. 'Those in favour of the Bluebell Hospice, raise your hand!' More typing.

Angel raised her hand, and most of the others followed suit, bar Adam, who still seemed put out on behalf of the pigs. Angel noticed Josh glance at Caspar again before raising his hand, and Caspar looked over at Angel, his face surprisingly serious, before at last he put his hand in the air too.

'The majority has it,' Olivia practically shouted, then sat down and began recording the event furiously on her computer.

'Great,' Tilda said. 'Angel and Caspar, hopefully you two will remember to actually come up with some ideas for what we're going to do for the fundraiser itself? Now, let's move on. Actually, I forgot to put something else on the agenda.' Olivia's eyes widened in shock, and Angel had to stifle a giggle. 'The school disco. We've been asked to come up with the theme this year!'

The group began to chatter excitedly, but Angel suddenly found herself watching Caspar – who was watching her back. She couldn't quite read the expression on his face. But one thing Angel did know was that working with Caspar to come up with fundraising ideas sounded even less fun than helping her elderly neighbour Miss Rosamund clean out her cat's litter tray.

As the bell rang for the next lesson, Angel heard a screech from behind her in the corridor that almost dislodged the only filling she had in her teeth.

'Aaangellll!'

She turned to see Izzy barrelling towards her, curls springing up and down spectacularly. Her best friend caught up with her breathlessly and then spun Angel around, urgently gripping her shoulders.

'Did. You see. My *texts*?' Izzy gasped. 'I could only message you this morning because *Mary* decided I shouldn't have been out so late the night before school. Said I should "decouple from my screen" for the evening and "dedicate more time to my studies". *Ugh*! Can you believe?'

Angel shook her head, tutting in sympathy at Izzy's struggles with her dad's *new wife* (Izzy deemed the word 'stepmother' to have too much 'mother' in it).

'But anyway? Did you?' Izzy continued.

Angel rummaged quickly in the pocket of her backpack. 'Sorry, Izz, I woke up late like I said, and then I had to go straight into the council meeting. Can you believe I have to work with *Caspar the-Only-Friendly-If-He-Thinks-You're-Cool, If-Only-He-Were-a-Ghost Johnson* to come up with ways to raise money for the charity this year? At least we've agreed that it's going to be the Bluebell, because they could really use—'

'Angel. Focus.'

Angel nodded, looking down at her phone to scroll through Izzy's messages. She saw the escalating giddiness of her friend recounting what had happened after Angel left the café yesterday evening. It amounted to: Izzy had gone up to the counter to order another mocha, but tripped over on her way back to her table, spilling her drink all

over herself, and her change everywhere. And . . .
Manny Patel had picked up a fifty pence piece and
handed it back to her.

'Err . . . wow.'

'Right? And he was like: "There you go." No,
wait. It was more like,' Izzy paused, lowering her
voice and quirking one eyebrow, ' "There you
go." ' Angel wasn't sure of the difference, but she
smiled at her friend encouragingly. 'Ange! It was
completely worth the minor burns and ruining my
favourite T-shirt.'

Angel couldn't help chuckling, but she was
beginning to find herself swept up in Izzy's
enthusiasm. And she didn't have the heart to
suggest Manny might have just been being polite.

'We're meant to be,' her friend concluded with
a nod, as though it was a done deal.

'That may be so, hon, but I've already been late
once this morning. We'd better get to chemistry
before Mr Howe starts pouring things into test tubes.'
Angel linked arms with Izzy, partly so that she could
spirit her friend down the corridor more quickly.

'Chemistry . . .' Izzy sighed dreamily. 'How appropriate!'

Angel wished she could feel the same way – but for now, she'd have to settle for the subject being strictly academic.

By the time the bell went for lunch, Angel was equal parts relieved and hungry. It had been hard work trying to concentrate on their Bunsen burners and complete their assigned chemistry experiment when she could feel Izzy bursting at the seams to talk more about Manny Patel. Grateful that their class was on first sitting for the canteen, Angel and Izzy headed to their favourite corner table after picking up their food, ready to dissect every syllable of Izzy's interaction with Manny with their other close friend, Ola. Today, Ola's tightly coiled hair had been braided into an elaborate crown on top of her

♥ 33 ♥

head – her mum was from Nigeria, and amazing at creating different styles. Ola's dad was Polish, and she loved giving a dramatic retelling of how her parents had found their daughter a name that was used, amazingly, in both their cultures. Ola viewed the story as painfully, utterly romantic, but then being theatrical was her thing. She had aspirations to be an actor.

The friends' lunchtime gossip session was interrupted by a couple of loud claps from Ms Gonzales, who was standing over by the dessert station where she clearly knew she'd most easily focus the students' attention. It *was* sticky toffee pudding day, after all.

'Guys, quiet down for a moment, please,' she called. 'As you know, it's that time of year again – those of you who've opted into our Secret Santa scheme this year, get ready to spread some clandestine joy!'

Angel, Izzy and Ola glanced at one another with broad smiles. Pretty much everyone loved Secret Santa. It was a really big deal at their school – people gave each other little gifts through the whole month of December. Angel heard the boys on Caspar's table whoop and rub their hands together with glee, eyeing some of the nearby girls. Her heart sank a little – she'd almost forgotten about the fact that Secret Santa also seemed to be an opportunity for matchmaking for a lot of her fellow students. As far as she was concerned, there was no point trying to trade names with people. It defeated the whole point! *And that, Angel Green, is why studying for scholarships occupies more of your time than the vague possibility of some kind of love life* . . . she told herself.

Still, people crowded in to pick out names from Ms Gonzales' Santa sack, and Angel couldn't help but get swept up in the excitement of seeing whose name she'd pull out as she edged closer and stuck her hand in . . .

Josh Yorke.

Hmm. Angel had known Josh almost as long as she'd known Caspar, but since the boys got popular when everyone started secondary school, she hadn't really hung around with them much at all. Now, not only did she have to brainstorm fundraising ideas with Caspar, but she had to think of Secret Santa gifts to give to his best mate in the lead up to Christmas, too! *Great*.

'Who'd you get?' Izzy asked Angel as they all returned to their tables. Angel showed her friend the slip of paper with a shrug as Izzy unfurled her own.

'Wait. This could defo be a sign,' she said, turning the piece of paper around to show Angel and Ola the name on it – Sanj Patel. 'It's like the universe is saying Sanj is going to be my brother-in-law, right? I'll have to think of some good gifts for him, and then maybe . . .'

Angel tuned out again, feeling only a little bit guilty, as she watched some of her fellow students in the canteen begin to trade names in a pretty obvious manner. There was a flurry of activity at the table next to Caspar's as girls loudly whispered his name, clearly vying for the opportunity to get him secret – or not so secret – gifts. Angel felt another eye-roll coming on.

❄

Angel was genuinely surprised to find that she didn't have to wait long for *her* first Secret Santa gift. Izzy and Ola had headed to the girls' loos in a time-honoured twosome to touch up their mascara – as subtly as they could get away with before Mrs Black told them off – but Angel headed to her locker. As she grabbed her stuff for afternoon lessons, she saw something wrapped in shiny paper, about the size of an A4 notebook, nestled at the bottom. After checking inside her bag for her wallet and other precious items (OK, mainly her study notes for the scholarship exam), she wondered who had been so organised that they had got her a gift on the very first day – not to mention figuring out her locker combination! She was curious to find out what the gift might be.

Knowing she had a few minutes before the next bell, Angel shut her locker and ducked out of the doors to head towards the benches in the break-out area in front of the school, sucking in a sharp breath at the cool December air. She sat down and looked at the tag on the gift. It seemed to be hand-made out of thick, red card.

To Angel. Love, Secret Santa.

Angel smiled, feeling oddly excited and touched that someone had taken the time to do all this. Had they also arranged things so that they definitely got to be her Secret Santa? That had never happened to her before!

Setting her bag beside her on the bench, she carefully undid the tape holding the wrapping paper together, and pulled out . . .

'Oooh, what did you get?' Izzy and Ola had spotted her through the double doors. 'God, it's freezing, isn't it?' Izzy added, walking around to the other side of the bench and rubbing her hands up and down her arms. 'I can't believe you've got a pressie already. Someone must have swapped so they could be your Secret Santa! Come on, what is it?'

Angel turned over the elaborately decorated gift, which also looked like someone had made it themselves. At first she was a bit disappointed, but then she studied it more closely. At the top of it was written: **Angel's Christmas Challenge Calendar**. 'Oh . . . I think it's an advent calendar?' she told her friends.

'Is there any chocolate in it?' Ola enquired hopefully.

Angel chuckled. 'Doesn't look like it.' She scanned the surface of the calendar and found the number one. 'It's covered with wax. I think you scratch the days off? Hey, Izz, can I borrow that fifty pence Manny retrieved for you?'

She and Ola laughed at Izzy's horrified face. Angel was sure that coin was enshrined in a frame in Izzy's bedroom by now. Ola handed her a two pence piece, and Angel scratched off the first day on her calendar.

Smile at everyone you see today.

What the heck? Angel shrugged and grinned maniacally up at the girls.

'Err, creepy,' Izzy said, just as the bell went.

It was a strange idea – and Angel wasn't convinced she wouldn't have preferred the usual chocolate advent calendar – but she decided she'd at least try to complete the challenges. Someone had put in the effort to make it. And it wasn't in her nature not to carry out a task that was set for her.

Angel managed to keep up her friendly facial assault all through double English (she figured one smile served as enough per person she made eye-contact with). It was actually kind of fun. She hadn't realised how little she smiled at people until she saw their looks of surprise at her greeting. Their pleased reactions were starting to make her feel quite good. Everyone started packing up their stuff as the end of maths – and of the day – rolled around, with plans of post-school activities. Angel maintained her smiles as she headed down the corridor to meet her friends and walk home. That was, until she saw someone was heading towards her. For some reason she didn't want to fail in her calendar's challenge, especially on day one, so reluctantly she turned a brief smile Caspar Johnson's way.

Caspar responded with a widening grin of his own, feigning to look around him as though he wasn't sure who hers was directed at. Angel continued striding past him, but Caspar changed direction to catch up with her. 'Um, Angel, I'm thinking we need to start working out some ideas for this fundraiser thing, right? Tilda sat next to me in geography, and she was talking about it a fair bit, so maybe . . . Do you have half an hour or something to have a quick catch up about it now? If we're doing the hospice, we want to make sure we come up with something pretty good . . .' He'd stopped near the lockers, leaning against one and looking down at Angel with a weird earnestness as she too came to a halt. She was vaguely aware of a couple of girls whispering to each other – probably shocked that Caspar Johnson was showing someone like her any attention at all.

'I suppose so,' she said, glancing down at her phone. She tapped out a quick message to Izzy that she would speak to her later, and her friend sent back a thumbs-up emoji.

'Don't sound *too* enthusiastic,' Caspar said sarcastically, pushing away from the locker he was leaning on. 'Anyway, I know one of the art rooms is free, we could duck in there?'

Angel shrugged and nodded, feeling suddenly a bit awkward as she walked beside Caspar back towards the classrooms. She remembered to smile – half-heartedly – at the stragglers wandering past them with curious looks, and Caspar held the door of one of the rooms open. They went in, and she heard him sigh as he dropped his bag down on one of the tables as though he was relieved to be in there. He wandered over to where a piece of thick paper was hanging from a line, testing the paint on its surface with his finger and nodding to himself. Angel hadn't seen the calm, contented look on his face before, and without thinking she moved to stand next to him, looking up at the intricate, abstract patterns of paint on the paper.

'That's great,' she found herself saying. 'Did you make that?'

Caspar glanced down at her, and Angel could have sworn that for a split second he actually looked . . . *shy?* The look was gone just as quickly though. 'What, you thought I just did finger painting or something, didn't you?' he said. She pursed her lips, but they stayed shoulder to shoulder for just a moment longer, looking at Caspar's painting, then back at each other.

'So . . . erm, fundraising ideas,' Angel said, feeling her face heat inexplicably. She turned away, rooting around in her bag for a notebook, then sat down on one of the stools by the nearest table. Caspar picked up a stray paintbrush and straddled one of the stools opposite her, running the brush's bristles up and down his palm absently, like it soothed him. Though Angel couldn't imagine why *he'd* need soothing ... 'What about a massive general knowledge quiz that people can sign up for?' she suggested. She warmed to the idea. 'Ooh, or, like, a maths olympics or spelling marathon or something, to find out who'll come out on top?'

Caspar attempted and completely failed to stifle a laugh. 'Believe it or not, AG,' he said, 'not everyone finds the idea of having to swot up even more than they do already fun.' He used air quotes as he said 'fun', and she felt a combination of irritation and embarrassment warm her face now. Angel frowned. 'We need people to actually want to participate, or we won't raise any money,' Caspar continued. He paused for a moment, thinking, and in spite of herself Angel found herself slightly mesmerised watching him move the paintbrush up and down the length of his hands. Caspar's hands looked kind of strong and ... *at home* with a brush gripped between his fingers. It suited him. Suddenly he stopped playing with the brush, snapping those fingers almost right in front of Angel's face before she'd remembered to retort to his sarky comments. *Ah. Back to supremely annoying, as usual.*

'Actually, a proper marathon's not a bad idea . . . What about a Christmas fun run or something?'

Angel pursed her lips and shook her head, pleased she could shoot down his idea too. 'It's freezing out there, in case you hadn't noticed?' Then, turning away from him, she decided she should at least write down the ideas they'd come up with in case Tilda needed evidence, even if so far they were getting nowhere. She frowned as she saw the handle of Caspar's paintbrush sneaking in between her braids, lifting them away from where they'd fallen in her face as she looked down at her notebook.

'Err, knock knock? You in there, AG?' Caspar enquired.

She swatted him away with a sigh. 'We need a better idea. Something fun for everyone.'

'You don't say.'

She ignored him. 'Something . . . I dunno, Christmassy.'

Caspar smirked, and she could tell the next idea out of his mouth would be stupid. 'Like a snog-a-thon under the mistletoe?' His eyes lingered a bit too long on Angel's, like a challenge. She fought every instinct to look away, instead staring Caspar down even as her face started to heat again.

'Be serious, for once?'

'What?' Caspar protested. 'People – well, most people – like to kiss . . .'

Angel finally looked away. The idea of a snog-a-thon sounded like something out of a cheesy romantic comedy film. Or maybe she was just getting embarrassed at the direction the brainstorm was heading. But actually—

'What about a film night?' Angel said suddenly. 'Christmas films! People love that. We can do snacks, and a different movie every week in the run-up to the end of term?'

Caspar chuckled and sat back, folding his arms. 'That's actually pretty good, you know, Angel.' He leaned forward again, resting his elbows on the table, his eyes sparkling. 'Hey, we could make new versions of the movie posters to put up around the school – maybe even sell a couple if people like them? I'd be up for making them.'

Angel was surprised they'd actually managed to come up with something they could agree on. 'Sounds good. Maybe we could make a list of what films—' she began, but Caspar's phone started to ping with messages, and as he pulled it out of his pocket to read them, he swore softly under his breath, frowning.

'Err, got to go,' he said, still frowning as he grabbed his bag. 'See you tomorrow.'

He was out of the door before Angel could even respond. Typical – the minute they got anything done, he was ready to give up and move on.

'I'll write up our ideas then,' Angel mumbled to herself, gathering her stuff and heading out. As she passed the caretaker in the hallway, he nodded at her.

'Hi, Mr Lewis,' she said.

'Angel – turn that frown upside down, eh?'

Angel had totally forgotten about her advent calendar challenge! She made a valid effort to smile, but from the dubious look on Mr Lewis's face, she wasn't sure she was successful. She'd have to start afresh with her new challenge tomorrow . . .

CHAPTER 4

Tuesday 2nd December

Angel's eyes sprang open at the sound of her phone's alarm going off – swiftly followed by a piercing, ringing noise from across the room: her mum's discarded, truly ancient analogue alarm clock, which came complete with the old-school bells on top.

'All right, all right!' she mumbled, untangling herself from her duvet, flopping on to the floor, and crawling across her small rug to switch it off. Angel had only herself to blame – the extra alarm had been her master plan for making sure she wouldn't risk being late today. She looked up as her mum opened her bedroom door and stared down at Angel sprawled on the carpet with the old clock gripped desperately between her hands.

'I won't ask,' Ruth said, her eyes twinkling with mirth. She was already dressed in her blue scrubs, with her favourite cosy purple cardigan over the top of them. 'I'm off now, darling. If you get in before me this evening, can you run the vacuum around a bit? Especially if you're going to be hanging about on the floor a lot,' she added with a chuckle.

'Har har. Yes, Mum, will do. Have a good day.'

Ruth came over to plant a quick kiss on her cheek, then headed off. Angel stood up and opened her curtains to the bright, frosty morning. Her eyes settled on her Secret Santa advent calendar propped up on the window sill. 'Suppose I should see what this has got in store for me today,' she said to herself, grabbing a coin off her desk to scratch away the next waxy disc. She hoped she wasn't going to regret her decision to embrace the advent calendar's challenges – she had enough on her plate already.

Try three things you've never done before.

Hmm, Angel thought. That should be fairly easy – she wasn't usually what anyone might call adventurous. But considering she was just going to school as normal, Angel wasn't sure what she might encounter today that was outside the usual. She got ready for school, and decided, after much internal debate, to put on two different coloured socks.

'Start small, Ange,' she said to herself with a self-deprecating laugh. One thing ticked off the list, at least!

She met Izzy on the high street, and they went into the Crafty Cuppa to buy their usual mocha (Izzy) and hot chocolate (Angel) before school. Angel considered doing her next 'never done before' thing by ordering a different drink, but she'd seen how buzzy even a little bit of coffee made Izzy, and she wasn't sure she was quite ready for that experience herself so early in the morning!

'Do you know you've not got matching socks on?' Izzy asked as they sipped their steaming-hot drinks gingerly, walking along to the school.

Angel laughed. 'I'm trying out some new stuff,' she replied.

'Ooh, speaking of which,' Izzy said, 'how did it go last night with your favourite over-popular footballer? Got an idea for the fundraiser yet?'

Angel shrugged, remembering the weirdness of yesterday after school with Caspar. 'We did come up with something, but then he legged it straight away. So annoyingly typical.'

Izzy nodded sympathetically, but then sped up a bit as she noticed someone crossing the road. 'Ooh, look – there's Sanj!' she said eagerly, even starting to wave. Angel chuckled to herself. So it took Izzy spotting her so-called future brother-in-law to actually get a wriggle on for their walk to school? Useful to know! She was a little bit surprised to notice that Sanj was walking along next to Josh, both of them talking animatedly and gesturing to a book Sanj was carrying. She hadn't known they were friends . . . Suddenly, Angel remembered she was meant to be finding out what Josh was into these days, so she could have a hope of figuring out what to get him for his first Secret Santa gift. She had a feeling he might have moved on from fidget spinners and Transformers.

Angel and Izzy caught up with the boys, and Angel cringed as Izzy went into super-sucking-up mode with Sanj. 'I *love* your scarf so much, by the way. Like, I've never seen one like that.'

'Err, thanks,' Sanj said, aiming a friendly smile at Angel, too. She surreptitiously tried to get a peek at the book Sanj was carrying, but he tucked it away inside his leather knapsack. At this rate, she had a feeling she might have to get something generic for Josh's first Secret Santa gift. But Angel Green didn't give up easily. If she could study for exams, surely she could study Josh until she figured out an idea for a gift.

'Hey, Josh,' she said, sidling up to him and attempting to check out the badges he'd pinned to his backpack for any clues.

'Hi, Angel. How's it going?'

'Yeah, good, good . . .' She spied something that looked like a football team-related badge, but she definitely had no idea which one. 'Seen any good, erm, matches lately?' OK, she was definitely coming across as weird, now!

'Mmmhmm. Last weekend . . . I didn't know you were into football? I seem to remember coming round to Cas's when we were kids to watch a match, and you went on about how stupid it was to chase a ball up and down the grass for ninety minutes?'

Trust Josh to choose now to actually remember stuff like that. He smiled at her, and she retorted, 'I mean, I was eight. But I might have had a point.'

They both laughed.

'I remember your hair being in braids back then, too, but shorter. These ones really suit you!' Josh said.

Angel pushed her hair out of her eyes to squint over at Josh in the wintery sunlight.

'Thanks!' she began with a smile. 'I—'

'Hey.'

Angel heard a deep, familiar voice interrupt behind them. She turned to see Caspar – but his expression was without his usual smirk as he looked between Angel and Josh. It was actually closer to a frown.

'Hey, mate,' Josh said, turning to look at Caspar too – with some degree of relief, Angel thought, trying not to be offended! The boys bumped fists, and Angel felt obliged to leave them to it. She went over to rescue Sanj from Izzy's over-eager clutches. Her friend was giving the poor boy the third degree about Manny's favourite doughnut flavour.

'We should be getting to English before the bell goes, eh?' Angel said, linking arms with Izzy as she was mid-flow about different types of jam fillings. 'See you later, Sanj!'

'Give my love to Manny,' Izzy said, and Angel squeezed her friend's arm tighter. 'Err, I mean . . . well, you know what I mean . . .'

Angel thought she heard Sanj chuckle and mutter that it was hard to miss her meaning. She turned to give a polite wave to Josh – and, grudgingly, Caspar. They waved back, and Angel thought she saw that same slightly subdued expression on Caspar's face. He looked maybe even a bit tired. Again, Angel found herself wondering if everything was OK with him . . . And then felt weird for wondering. She shook herself out of it, thinking instead about giving her English essay a final once-over before the lesson started. She had to stay focussed!

'But . . . But nobody *actually* chooses the liver and onions . . .'

Angel chewed, swallowed, then grimaced, watching Ola and Izzy's horrified faces across the canteen table at lunchtime. *Thing She'd Never Done Before* Number Two was already becoming the thing Angel was sure she'd regret the most in her whole entire life. Still, she valiantly cut up another piece of liver, trying not to think about it too much.

'It tastes . . .' *Of bad decisions.* 'Not that bad.' She took a long glug of her Coke, then sat back from her plate for a moment. She looked over to the popular boys' table, and noticed that Josh was watching something on his phone. Maybe whatever it was might give her a Secret Santa gift clue? 'Err, I'm just going to grab some salt and pepper,' she told her friends, standing up to walk surreptitiously past Josh's table. Edging closer, she jumped as someone said her name.

'Angel?' Caspar said bemusedly, and her eyes snapped up as she was leaning over Josh's shoulder. 'Considering a career in espionage? I'm gonna say, stick to medicine.'

Angel flushed as Josh turned around to look at her, too. She stood up straighter. At least she'd noticed that it was some kind of snowboarding video he was watching. Not that it gave her the foggiest idea what to actually get as a gift – ski equipment was definitely above the price limit. But it was something!

'Thanks for the tip,' Angel replied sarcastically to Caspar's jibe, seeking her escape towards the little bank of condiments, cutlery and seasoning nearby. But she was intercepted by Tilda and Olivia striding towards them. Well, *Tilda* was striding, with her usual determined look on her face. Olivia could be better described as trailing along behind her.

'Ah, Angel, Caspar, glad I caught you,' Tilda said, coming to a halt in front of Caspar's table and folding her arms. 'Have you sorted out what we're going to do for the Bluebell Hospice fundraiser?'

Angel stifled a giggle as she saw Olivia's eyes widen in alarm. 'B-but we're outside the official council meeting,' she whispered to Tilda, scrambling in her bag for her notebook to take down their conversation.

'We have, as it happens,' Caspar interjected, standing up. He put one arm around Angel's shoulder and squeezed. For one tiny second, being nestled into his strong shoulder actually felt kind of . . . good? Ugh! Angel swiftly ducked away from under his arm, pulling a face. All she needed was him mocking her.

'Is that right?' Tilda asked, turning her attention to Caspar fully and actually seeming to flutter her lashes a bit.

'Yeah,' Angel said quickly, pulling the girl's gaze back in her direction, and pursing her lips as she shook her head at Caspar. He grinned back at her infuriatingly, of course. 'We're thinking movie night. Charge for tickets, snacks and stuff.'

Olivia's pen looked like it would set her page on fire as she took down her notes, but she was nodding. 'That's actually a really good idea,' she said, then looked over to Tilda for affirmation. 'Right?'

'Yes. I like it,' Tilda said, unfolding her arms – but only so she could put her hands on her hips. She smiled up at Caspar, then nodded once at Angel, her grin fading. 'Cool. Get cracking with it, we'll get updates at the next council meeting.' With that, she turned on her heel and strode away. Olivia remained a moment longer to record that, then waved goodbye too as Caspar chuckled cockily.

Angel made to move away and grab her seasonings at last, but Caspar reached out and held her arm lightly for a moment before quickly letting his hand drop away, as though he was grossed out by touching her or something. She pursed her lips.

'Look, Angel, I was thinking . . .' he began. 'I was going to make a start on the posters tonight, get going on some screen prints so we have enough to start putting up around the school. Seeing as we need to decide which film we want to go for first, maybe you should help me out with the posters after school, too?' His hazel eyes were wide and focussed on her, and Angel felt her heart quicken a bit at the attention – not least because, as ever, Caspar Johnson came with an audience of girls (and some guys) watching his every move. He briefly ran his hands over those afro curls, making them spring back into place. He was staring at her. Because . . . she wasn't replying!

'Err . . . I had kind of put tonight aside to do some more studying for my scholarship exam . . .' Angel began, but then she remembered the advent calendar, and that she still had one thing she'd never done before to tick off if she was to fulfil today's challenge. Making movie posters would certainly be better than eating liver and onions, even if it would involve spending another evening with Caspar.

'Of course you had,' he said, folding his arms. 'I mean this was dumped on *both* of us, you know. There's loads of other stuff I'd rather be doing, but—'

Angel held up a hand, which she then used to flip her braids away from her face, and Caspar stopped grumbling. 'All right, all right. Go on then,' she said, 'as long as you don't plan to run off again.' She raised an eyebrow, and he gave a half-smile that at least had the decency to be a tiny bit bashful. As much as someone that arrogant could look even vaguely embarrassed, anyway. He shook his head and the look was gone.

'Shouldn't be a problem,' he said, slapping on that winning grin that she'd seen make other girls swoon. Angel thought she could hear a couple of them simpering behind her. 'See you then,' he concluded. 'Same room as last night.'

Angel nodded. 'Cool, see you then.'

She walked away, hearing whispers follow her through the canteen back to Izzy and Ola at their table. But no, Caspar Johnson *wasn't* asking Angel Green out – this was strictly council business, she thought, grimacing as she sat down to her cold plate of liver. Angel returned to chatting to her friends, but her thoughts drifted to her plans for after school. She actually kind of felt, in some completely weird way, like she might be . . . looking forward to it?

CHAPTER 5

He was late. Of course he was. Angel had already sat in the art room like a Muppet while Mr Thomas, one of the maths teachers, looked in on her with a puzzled expression asking if everything was OK, and a Year Seven who claimed to have forgotten where the loos were burst in then swiftly out again. Fifteen minutes later, Angel heard some boys' voices outside the door. It was Caspar, at last, saying bye to his mates loudly.

The door opened, and Angel felt her face form into a frown of irritation, but it morphed into one of confusion as she saw that Caspar was covering his eyes with one hand, a smug smile nestled below it.

'Now, let me guess . . . Arms folded, brows knitted, braids falling in your eyes . . .' He released his hand, his grin widening as he pointed at Angel in exactly the stance he had described. She unfolded her arms quickly. He had got her there.

'Sorry I'm late,' Caspar continued, dumping his bag on a table and pulling something out of it, 'but I can't do any kind of real art without snacks!'

Angel's eyes went from narrowed to wide as the English Channel when she saw what he was holding out to her. 'Whoa, where did you find those?' she said, grabbing the bag of sweets out of Caspar's hand. They were the space-themed sour chewy sweets of pure deliciousness that they had gorged on as kids. She hadn't seen them for years!

Caspar tapped his nose conspiratorially. 'I have my sources . . .'

'The internet, right?' she said with a short laugh, and he nodded, chuckling too. She opened the packet without thinking.

'Oh, help yourself, AG,' he said, and she froze, but he shook his head and grabbed a couple himself. Simultaneously they screwed their faces up for a moment as the sourness of the confection hit their tongue, then sighed in pleasure. Angel felt like she was eight years old again. It was a weird sensation – especially when she looked over and definitely didn't see an eight-year-old Caspar looking back at her. He was a lot . . . taller now.

'Thanks,' she mumbled.

'Sorry, what was that?'

She pursed her lips, and snatched another sweet from the packet with a wry expression. 'I said thanks.'

Caspar mimed having a heart attack, clutching his chest and stumbling backwards, then, laughing to himself, he went over to one of the big drawers at the back of the classroom. 'OK, so we should get some supplies together and decide what we want to do on the posters,' he said. 'I'm thinking if we do lino cuts, we can print lots of the same image, in different colours and stuff.'

Angel was surprised at how engaged Caspar seemed when it came to stuff like this. Most of the time at school he didn't seem that fussed, always ready to crack a joke or cause some distraction. She knew this was just his way of avoiding anything vaguely academic, but he seemed to be in his element in the art room – it was unexpected, to say the least.

'Sounds good,' Angel said, walking over to the table where Caspar was starting to set down supplies. 'But we should probably figure out what film we're going to screen for our first showing. How about . . . *It's a Wonderful Life*?'

Caspar grimaced and waved his hands in dissent exaggeratedly, shaking his head. 'That super-depressing old black and white one? Uh-uh, absolutely not. You tried to make us watch that one time when I was over your house when we were kids, and even your mum and dad weren't having it!'

Angel pretended to be annoyed, but she found herself hiding a chuckle. 'I maintain it's a good Christmas movie. You just have to keep going with it.'

Caspar raised an eyebrow. 'It needs to be something that will appeal to people born this *century*,' he said. 'You just like the fact that there's a guardian angel in it. But since we'll have you, *Angel*, we should think of something else. If it makes you feel better, I'll make you some wings to wear while you sell the snacks.'

Angel balled up a stray bit of crepe paper from the table and flicked it at him. 'Who says I'll be the one doing the selling? Anyway, fine. What do you suggest, then?'

Caspar laid out a piece of the lino, thinking. 'I seem to remember that same Christmas you had another favourite – you kept singing that Mariah Carey song like the little American girl in it does . . .'

She was genuinely surprised he remembered that. '*Love, Actually*. Yes! Good idea.'

'Your voice wasn't half bad back then,' Caspar continued, beginning to sketch an image out on the lino, avoiding her eye. 'Do you still sing?'

The question blindsided Angel a bit. She'd been so focussed on studying lately, completely consumed by the idea that down the line she'd become a doctor. She hadn't really given much thought to her original, hairbrush-gripping childhood dream of being the next R 'n' B diva! She drew a breath without even thinking about it, and let rip with a few lines of the song from the film.

Caspar stared at her for a moment, then broke into a sudden, wide smile that Angel couldn't help but mirror. He nodded and began to clap, and she flushed, bowing dramatically and striking a diva pose. 'Still got it, I suppose,' she mumbled, more than a little embarrassed. She couldn't quite believe she'd done it, but since Caspar was showing her his artistic side, maybe that was what had encouraged her. She'd probably gone over her limit of new things for the day!

Caspar returned to the lino, and Angel went to look over his shoulder. He'd made a really cool, graphic image of Christmassy themes that tied in to the film – he'd obviously just drawn from his memory. 'Want me to show you how to make a lino cut?' he asked.

Angel swept her braids over her shoulder from where she'd been looking down to study his drawing, and found herself surprisingly close to Caspar. 'Yeah, go on then,' she said softly. Then, feeling the need to break the moment, she stretched over to grab another sweet and began chewing emphatically. Caspar picked up one of the lino blades he'd pulled out of a little case in his bag. He held it out to her, but then quickly pulled it back again.

'Hmm ... do I trust you with this is the question?' he said with a mock-frown. 'That scowl earlier was bordering on homicidal ...'

'Har har. Hand it over,' Angel said, and he placed the handle in her palm. She tried to ignore the little spark of electricity she felt as his fingers brushed her hand.

'Actually, my lino blades are a bit blunt,' Caspar said absently. 'I keep meaning to get some new ones ...' Nevertheless, he took up another of the blades and began carefully cutting away the image. Angel watched as he concentrated, then realised she was looking at his face and not what he was showing her. 'The parts you cut away are the parts you *don't* want printed,' Caspar was explaining, and she tried to focus. 'Want to try it?'

Angel tentatively took up the tool he'd handed to her, and it was surprisingly satisfying to cut away at the linoleum. She grinned as she worked, but found her hair was getting in the way. Tutting, she paused and rummaged in her pencil case for an elastic band.

'Is that what you're going to use?' Caspar asked her as she quickly caught some of her braids back off her face. 'I'm only asking because my mum gets braids put in sometimes. She says it's easier to take care of, especially when Ruby . . .'

Angel glanced at him. Caspar hardly ever mentioned his little sister. She must be five or six now, born around the time Angel and Caspar had drifted apart. Of course, Angel had been distracted by losing her dad by then, too. But she remembered something about the little girl having some health problems. 'Well,' Caspar continued quickly, 'when Mum's taking care of my sister and running around, whatever.' He turned back to the lino cutting with a renewed concentration. 'Anyway, she's always going on about not using things that snag on them. Her braids, I mean,' he finished in a mumble.

Angel chuckled. 'Well, thanks for the hair tips, Johnson. That's true, but for now I'll have to work with what I've got.'

Caspar was still cutting, and sat up eventually as he finished. 'There,' he said, seeming relieved to move on from the beauty talk. 'Now we're ready to ink.'

As they worked on a few poster prints in different colours, weirdly Angel couldn't help thinking that she hadn't felt so chilled out in weeks – probably months even. It was nice to concentrate on something that wasn't a textbook for once. She was actually glad that her Secret Santa's advent calendar had persuaded her to try something different. *Speaking of which* ... Since she had

Caspar as a captive audience, Angel decided she might as well ask him more about Josh, to see if she could finally come up with an idea for a gift.

'Hey,' she asked, and Caspar looked over at her. 'Obviously I haven't hung out with you lot for a while, so I'm a bit out of touch . . .'

Caspar nodded. 'Yeah, this is a bit like old times. I think—' he began, but Angel pressed on.

'Actually, I was going to ask – what's *Josh* into these days? It's so hard to know what—'

'Josh?' Caspar's mouth seemed to tighten a bit as he turned away and began to hang up the poster prints to dry. 'You'd have to ask him,' he muttered.

Just like that, the good vibe of the evening felt like it had been ruined – and Angel wasn't sure if it was her fault or Caspar's. Maybe they just weren't destined to get along any more.

'Yeah. Maybe I will,' she said, stifling a sigh.

For the second time, she felt a weird combination of happy, confused and disappointed as she left the art room that evening and headed home.

CHAPTER 6

Wednesday 3rd December

The next morning, Angel was up early, planning to munch on some cereal and catch up on the studying she hadn't been able to do last night before she had to head to school. But panic gripped her as she realised she couldn't find her laptop *anywhere*. It had taken months of payments for her and her mum to afford it. Where could she have left it?

She rushed down the narrow staircase in their house, heart pounding, but as she rounded the corner she saw someone sitting at their little dining table, glasses perched on her nose as she peered at the screen, then grinning and typing something.

'Err, Mum? What are you doing? You almost gave me a heart attack wondering where my computer was!' Angel exclaimed, hands on her hips.

Her mother looked at Angel over the frames of her glasses, eyebrows raised. Angel immediately relaxed her stance. 'Sorry, *whose* computer?' her mum enquired, eyebrows still reaching up towards the hairline of her neat afro.

'*The* computer,' Angel corrected herself grudgingly. 'I was going to do a bit of research for the scholarship exam before school.' Her mum was never usually one to surf the internet or email anyone. As Angel edged around Ruth to get to the kitchen and grab a bowl out of the cupboard, she caught a glance at the screen. Her mum seemed to be on a chat app with—

'Victor sent me a link on here, and then we ended up chatting a bit and—' Ruth broke off as a notification popped up, and gave the screen another grin before beginning a one-finger-typed reply. 'Sorry, darling, I'll be off in just a mo.'

So her mum was still chatting to This Victor? Angel was starting to think she ought to meet the bloke, check him out. Her mum seemed really into him, which Angel *supposed* was a good thing, but it was hard to wrap her head around. But what if this man wanted to move in here? Or *marry* her mum? What if he had kids of his own? What if—

'Angel Green, those cornflakes don't grow on trees, you know,' her mum said, closing the laptop with a flourish and gesturing to where Angel was tipping almost the whole packet of cereal into her bowl. Angel quickly retrieved the scattered flakes back into the packet and sat down, sliding the computer over in front of her and opening it. She was slightly grossed-out at the idea she might see whatever her mum was typing to her new bae.

Swallowing a grimace, Angel tried to sound casual as she asked, 'So, you've been chatting to This Victor a fair bit . . . How did you . . . I mean, is he . . .?'

Her mum pulled the bottle of orange juice out of the fridge, and poured each of them a glass. She sat down at the table with Angel, looking into her drink for a moment. *Wow, this must be serious*, Angel thought . . . Until her mum said, 'Oh, looks like I got the kind with bits, sorry, love. I know you don't like feeling you have to chew your juice.' She chuckled, and Angel couldn't help smiling too. 'Listen, it's true, I have been talking to Victor a fair bit.' Her face really did turn contemplative this time. 'He's a lovely gentleman I met at work when he came to fix the computer at the reception desk and . . .'

Angel actually thought her mum might be blushing!

'He's a charming one, it has to be said.' Ruth looked at Angel. 'But it's all very new, it's nothing serious just yet. It's hard, you know, even after all these years . . .' She trailed off. If Angel knew one thing, it was that her mum never really liked to talk about her dad. Sometimes she wished Ruth would. Her mum cleared her throat. 'He said he'd like to take me out at the weekend, so I thought I'd see if we get on before I introduced you and—'

Angel nodded, and did her best to smile. 'You should, Mum. I mean, I'll be running a background check before you do though, make sure he's not too obviously dodgy or anything! What did you say his surname was?' Angel opened the search engine on the computer, fingers poised to type.

'I didn't,' her mum said pointedly, but still smiling fondly. 'Now, didn't *you* say you had some work to do?' She drained her chewy juice and put her glass in the sink. 'Don't waste that cereal!' her mum concluded before she headed upstairs to get ready for work. 'And please—'

' "Wash those things up before you go," ' Angel finished with a laugh. *So predicable.* At least some things about her mum hadn't changed!

Angel scanned the shelves of the shop around the corner from school, keeping a close eye on the time, and grabbed a giant bag of sweets off the shelf. Chocolate balls covered in desiccated coconut and filled with some marshmallow-y goo – to be honest, she thought they sounded pretty disgusting, but it was the best she could come up with given the total £10 spending cap for gifts. Snowballs! They were kind of related to Josh's interests in winter sports, and she was pretty sure he'd still have a sweet tooth, too. She paid quickly, then crammed the chocolates into the gift bag she'd pilfered from her mum's stash before she left the house. Ruth Green didn't like to throw things like wrapping paper and gift bags away, and for once Angel was grateful. She hid the Secret Santa gift away in her bag. She'd just have to work out the best time to get it to Josh at some point during the day.

Feeling relieved that she'd at least figured out *something* to get, Angel rushed the rest of the way to school, remembering that Izzy had PE first thing this morning, so would definitely already be in the nurse's office feigning some kind of illness rather than waiting to meet her. Tilda had sent round a group message to the school council members calling for an interim meeting at lunchtime to discuss the fundraiser and the school disco plans, so Angel quickly messaged to let Izzy know they'd have to try catching up after school. She was definitely finished with wasting her evenings on Caspar Johnson. After getting home last night, Angel had spent a decent chunk of time online sorting out the special permission they had to get for screening a film at the school. At least she'd managed to forge ahead on her own after things had ended weirdly with her so-called co-organiser *once again*.

The morning's lessons went by in a flash, and before the lunchtime council meeting, Angel sped over to the canteen just as the first bell was going. She made sure to leave Josh's Secret Santa gift on the table where the boys usually sat, hoping nobody would either notice her doing it, or decide to be idiots and tuck into the chocolate themselves. Luckily, her stealth movements worked. As she slipped away, she saw Josh already over by the fridge full of sandwiches. Then the bag on his table seemed to catch his eye, and he went over to grab it. She was too nervous to stick around to see his reaction, though. She made her way to the council meeting in the usual classroom, but five minutes or so later, she was surprised to see Sanj enter the room munching on one of the 'snowballs'. She was pretty sure the canteen vending machine didn't sell them!

'Where did you get that?' she asked.

'Oh – Josh gave me one. Was his Secret Santa gift, I think,' Sanj replied, sitting down beside her. 'Not too bad, actually . . .'

OK good. At least they tasted all right . . . One present down, though Angel had no idea what else she might come up with. She unzipped her bag to grab her notebook before the meeting began, and was surprised to see something shiny nestling in the bottom of her backpack. How had she not noticed that before? She had a feeling, with a zip of excitement, that it might be *her* next Secret Santa present! She didn't really want to open it in front of everyone, but she was looking forward to seeing what it was later. The festive spirit was really in the air today! She remembered what her advent calendar had said when she scratched it off this morning:

Talk to someone you've never spoken to before.

Maybe she should continue with the momentum of all this Christmassy goodwill and see if she could tick off that challenge, too. *Hmm.* Angel looked around the room at the members of the council beginning to gather. No Caspar yet, of cour— Oh. She looked away quickly as she saw his broad shoulders fill the doorframe, followed by Josh, both of them munching on sandwiches from the canteen. Why hadn't she thought of grabbing something while she was there? Her stomach rumbled loudly, and she clutched it, embarrassed, then noticed Olivia carefully looking around the room to record the members in attendance. OK, Angel had exchanged one or two words with the officious second-in-command before, but nothing close to a real conversation. Calendar challenge accepted!

'Err, hey, Olivia. How's it going?'

Olivia looked up, smoothing her hair back behind her ears with a few swipes before appearing to jot down Angel's enquiry. 'Fine thanks,' she responded.

'I don't think we've ever really had a chance to chat,' Angel began. 'How are you finding being on the council this year?'

Olivia looked a little surprised at Angel striking up an actual conversation, and almost glad, which made Angel feel pretty good too, if also a bit ashamed that she'd never tried it before. This calendar actually had some good suggestions.

'I'm enjoying it,' Olivia said. 'It's nice to feel useful, you know?' She smiled, and Angel noticed how sweet it was. 'Even if it does mean missing out on lunch sometimes. It's burger and chips day today!'

Angel nodded. 'Yeah, I totally forgot to grab something, I'm starving!'

'You can have my other half if you like?' Angel turned, surprised to see Caspar proffering his sandwich wrapper, and notice that Josh had raised a surprised eyebrow, too. Caspar looked between them with a dismissive shrug. 'I'm not going to eat it. I mean, it does have mustard in it though, and I seem to remember an unfortunate, and very snotty, incident where Angel got some up her nose when we were seven—'

'Yeah, I'll manage without. Thanks,' Angel retorted sarcastically. She'd actually almost felt bad that she hadn't just accepted to begin with, but then, as usual, he'd had to ruin it anyway. What was his problem? It was like he was always trying to provoke her. It was silly to think they could ever be friends again. After all he'd abandoned her right when she needed him most when they were kids.

Thankfully Angel didn't have much time to dwell, as Tilda called the meeting to order. After a quick catch-up on the school disco planning, she turned to Angel and Caspar.

'Now, I hope you two have made some progress on the first fundraising event for the hospice?'

Angel opened her mouth to speak, but before she could say anything Caspar stood up, hoisted a big roll of papers onto the table in front of everyone, and flicked it to unfurl it with a flourish. 'We have!' he said, gesturing to the posters, then glancing down at Angel and giving her a smirk. She turned her gaze towards their work and then couldn't help giving him a grudging smile. The lino cuts had turned out amazingly, and Caspar had spent time block-printing the film title and the screening information on to them too. She almost had to stifle a 'wow'! 'My mate Yugo is ready to help us with the digital projection, too—'

'And I've sorted out the licence for the screening,' Angel interjected with a nod, standing up to speak to the rest of the council members beside Caspar. She couldn't let him do his usual tactic of charming everyone and taking all the credit. 'And I'm going to make some snacks for us to sell, as well.'

'Really? I mean, exactly,' Caspar said. They both sat down simultaneously, and Caspar nodded at her. She returned the nod grudgingly, while Tilda looked at the posters, clearly impressed.

'Nice work,' she said, and the others murmured their admiration too. Angel was a bit surprised they'd actually pulled this off. 'Can we grab some volunteers to help Caspar and Angel hang these posters up around the school? The sooner we can get the word out, the better . . .'

Sanj raised a hand. 'Happy to help.'

'Oh – yeah me, too,' Josh said, and for a second Angel thought she saw a brief smile pass between Sanj and Josh, before Caspar raised a fist for Josh to bump. Great, her and a bunch of boys.

But only a few moments after they got out into the hallway with the tape and posters, Izzy emerged, with her eyes focussed on Sanj, undoubtedly ready to talk his ear off about Manny some more. 'Need a hand, guys?' Izzy said. 'I'm *really* into volunteering for things, you know . . .' Angel knew her friend had recently learned Manny helped out at the local dog shelter, so Izzy had clearly decided she needed to up her philanthropic credentials. Somehow, Angel doubted word of her helping tear sticky tape would reach Sanj's older brother, but she was happy for her friend to join them.

'Angel?' she heard Caspar ask, and she turned to pass him a little piece of tape. His fingers were warm as he lifted it, and Angel found herself watching a bit too eagerly as Caspar stretched to hang a poster up high on one of the glass doors in the corridor, a sliver of the brown skin of his taut stomach peeking out above his belt. *Eugh. No. What was she thinking!*

She was very grateful when the final bell went, and she had just enough time to grab a veggie wrap in the canteen to munch on her way to French. Izzy joined her at the till, picking up a packet of sweets and batting her eyelids at Angel to pay for them alongside her food.

'I think Sanj is going to put in a good word for me with Manny,' Izzy said with a dreamy sigh.

Angel took a big bite of her wrap, and Izzy pulled a grossed-out face at her as she chewed contemplatively. She couldn't remember the last time she'd had a crush like the one Izzy was clearly deep into experiencing ... But then Angel wondered if her friend was maybe throwing herself into the whole Manny thing because things weren't so great elsewhere. Like, at home. Swallowing, she asked softly, 'How are things with the stepmonster?'

Izzy sighed an entirely different sigh this time. 'Not ... not amazing, to be honest, Ange. Something's going on. She's been acting fussier than usual, and Dad's treating her like she's made of glass. I have a feeling she might be ... *pregnant*.' They both grimaced at the thought of how that would have come about, and then Izzy's face fell again. 'Like Dad's attention isn't already on her enough, they'll have a kid of their own, and then who knows where that will leave me and Charly? Although my little sis will probably think it's great to have a younger sibling of her own to boss about.'

'You *have* been a great role model on that front,' Angel joked gently, but then reached out and squeezed her friend's shoulder. 'It'll be OK, Izz. Listen, why don't you come over to mine tomorrow after school? I could use a hand with these snacks for the film screening, and that could give you even more brownie points for the Manny Project, eh? Ooh, brownies . . .'

Izzy sniffed a little and smiled. 'Yeah, good call. As long as *you* don't get bossy on me about measuring.'

'*Moi?*' Angel feigned clutching a necklace of pearls, and they both giggled. 'Come on, let's get to class.'

CHAPTER 7

Thursday 4th December

At home after school, Angel pulled off her school jumper with relief, and tugged on her favourite hoody. She heard something fall to the floor and smiled as she bent over to pick it up. She adjusted her braids and slipped the silky headband around them again, pushing her hair back from her face and letting it fall around her shoulders. Looking at herself in the mirror, a little frown of puzzlement nestled back between her brows as she admired herself. Again, she wondered who could have given the hairband to her . . .

She'd got so swept up in the poster hanging and the rest of lessons yesterday afternoon that it was only when she'd got home and unpacked her textbooks from her bag that she'd remembered the shiny gift at the bottom. Sitting down on her bed for a second now, Angel picked up the tag that had been on the present from where it lay on her bedside table and re-read the note:

> Your face is too pretty to hide.
> Love, Secret Santa

'It *must* be Izzy,' she said out loud to herself. 'But wait, no, it can't be. She said she got Sanj for her Secret Santa. Ola . . .?' She turned the tag over in her hands. She definitely didn't recognise the handwriting, but whoever it was could have been sneaky and asked someone else to do it. The message was so nice, she almost thought it might be her mum or something, like when she sent Angel a Valentine's card every February pretending it was from a mystery admirer. But how would her mum have got into school, and into her locker, to give her the advent calendar? The message was almost . . . romantic? Angel felt embarrassed just thinking that. But the gift was really thoughtful, and whoever had given it to her was clearly ignoring the rule about the price cap . . .

The doorbell interrupted Angel's mental sleuthing.

'I'm ready to get *foody*!' Izzy announced as soon as Angel opened the door, with her friend undoing her duffle coat to reveal an apron that said *Kiss the chef* on it.

'Loving the enthusiasm,' Angel said with a laugh, stepping aside to let her friend in. She'd already gathered up the ingredients that she'd been able to buy using the school council's slush fund. 'Don't suppose you picked up some more vanilla essence when you went past the supermarket, like I messaged you to?'

Izzy cringed and shook her head. 'Oops.'

'Ugh, OK. We should have enough. Otherwise, you can always pop out again, eh?' Angel smiled brightly at her friend.

'But it's coooold,' Izzy said, taking off her coat, dropping it on to the sofa and then heading towards the radiator in the living room to perch her bottom on it. 'Besides,' she continued as her gaze alighted on Angel's advent calendar, which she'd left on the kitchen table, 'this thing says "Do something that's the opposite to your usual"' today! So like I told you, you have to be completely non-bossy!'

Angel gasped in mock-anger and threw a chocolate button in Izzy's direction, but she caught it in her mouth with a precision that Angel couldn't help but be impressed with. Izzy chewed smugly, and Angel chuckled.

'Fine, all right. Let's get going, eh?'

An hour later, Angel had done her best not to let the somewhat *controlling* side of her personality take over. It was definitely a challenge, given that Izzy had managed to turn the ancient electric mixer (which Angel was sure had been handed down from her grandma to her mum) on too high, sending icing sugar and flour flying around the kitchen. She'd then put green food colouring into the cupcake batter, but to be fair, then they decided to do another batch in red and make them 'festive'. Izzy had now settled down at the kitchen table, feet up, to eat an unsettling amount of the raw batter left over in the mixing bowl while the cakes baked. Angel shook her head to herself, and began heating up oil to start popping some corn for them to package up into little bags.

'I reckon it must be a secret admirer, you know, not just a Secret Santa,' Izzy said between slurping batter off her fingers, nodding at Angel's headband. 'That thing is so cute I might have to borrow it. Who could it be, d'you think?'

Angel bit her lip, dropping a kernel of corn into the oil to test it. It fizzled and popped, so she shook the bag into the big pot on the stove and put the lid on. 'I don't think it is an admirer, Izz. I mean, who would . . . It doesn't feel likely, you know?'

Izzy finally finished swiping her fingers around the bowl and brought it over to the sink. 'Don't be ridiculous, Ange! You? Are the cleverest person I know, for starters, not to mention being ten out of ten buff to boot. It's *completely* likely.' She eyed Angel sideways. 'What about Josh Yorke? I mean, I know you're his Secret Santa, but he might have made it so he got you, too?'

Angel pulled a face and shook her head. 'I don't think so.'

'Oh, or that other boy from the council ... Adam Clarke?'

Laughing, Angel went over to shake the pot, hearing the kernels begin to explode in satisfying pops. 'I think he's a bit too focussed on his family's pig farm to be interested in buying me thoughtful gifts,' she said. Lifting the lid with a flourish, she grinned over at Izzy, who immediately rushed over to place a warm piece of popcorn in her mouth.

'I know,' she said, but then paused. 'Wow. That was hot.' She swallowed. 'But hey, what about Ca—'

But Izzy's suggestion was interrupted by the sound of Angel's mum coming through the front door. 'Mmm, smells delicious in here, girls!' She put down her bags and shrugged off her coat, giving Angel a kiss and hugging Izzy warmly.

'It's for the first film screening we're doing as part of the fundraiser,' Angel explained, pulling the popcorn pot off the stove as the sound of popping kernels began to slow. 'You know, for the hospice.'

'Oh yes, of course.' Angel's mum smiled, crouching down to look through the oven door at the cakes baking. 'We could certainly use all the help we can get. These look fantastic!'

Izzy crouched beside Ruth, nodding. 'They do, don't they? Hard work whipping all this up, let me tell you, Ms Green!' Angel bit her tongue, remembering that she was meant to be doing the opposite of what she usually would. It was mighty difficult keeping her sarcastic comment to herself, but she just about managed it. 'Caspar Johnson is supposedly Angel's partner on all of this,' Izzy continued, 'but he's nowhere to be found, as usual.'

Angel's mum stood up and straightened out her scrubs, looking thoughtful. 'Hmm, well you never know what people have going on, eh? Brilliant that you've stepped in though, Izzy-Bee. I'd expect nothing less.'

Izzy beamed at Ruth's praise, and then flounced on to the sofa while Angel's mum went upstairs to change. Her friend didn't budge as the timer for the cakes went off, and Angel gave a wry smile as she fetched them out of the oven. Putting the cakes onto a rack on the table to cool, she noticed a pamphlet on top of her mum's things that caught her attention. It read: *St Teddington's Hospital – Inspiring Britain's Future Medics.*

Angel picked up the pamphlet just as her mum came back down the stairs in her favourite purple tracksuit and sheepskin slippers, eyeing the cakes hungrily. 'Oh, yes, darling, I got that for you. I know you're already cramming for the scholarship, but this is a one-day course where you get to shadow doctors at St Ted's. Get some real-life experience!'

Angel's eyes widened.

'And,' her mum continued, 'Dr Benedict at the

hospice helps run the scheme there, so she said she can fit you into a slot *next Saturday!* Those Dunstable Academy bods will definitely be impressed by that, right? I know it's short notice, but what do you think?'

Angel stared at her mum, then down at the brochure, then back at her mum. 'Um, what do I think?' A grin spread across her face and she launched herself at Ruth, squeezing her tight. 'I think you're the best mum in this hemisphere!'

Ruth chuckled even as she began tapping on Angel's shoulder, still locked in their embrace. 'A breath would be nice, sweetheart.'

Angel relaxed her grip, and Izzy finally lifted herself back off the sofa to come over to them. 'Only you would be excited about having to do more work on the weekend, Ange,' she said, but she smiled happily. 'Now, how are these cakes looking . . .?'

Angel smacked Izzy's hand away, but was too slow to stop her mum, who swooped in to scoop one up. 'Mmm . . .' Angel opened her mouth to protest, but her mum pointed at herself and mumbled, 'Best mum in the hemisphere, remember?' between cakey chews.

Angel hadn't thought the day could get any better after her Secret Santa gift, but this was going to be amazing! She couldn't wait until next Saturday. But for now she had to focus on tomorrow – and their first fundraiser film screening!

CHAPTER 8

Friday 5th December

Yawning as she dusted a final layer of sprinkles over the iced cupcakes, Angel gratefully accepted the cup of tea her mum set by her on the counter the next morning.

'I'm very proud of you, sweetheart. These are great. Everyone at the hospice really appreciates the effort you guys are putting in to raise money for us.'

Ruth was in her dressing gown still, sipping her own cup of tea, and Angel was glad to see that she was finally taking the day off. Even when she wasn't on a shift, her mum often went in to the hospice anyway. She was *dedicated*. Angel wanted to be just like her when it came to looking after people as a doctor.

'Mum,' she began, suddenly wondering something, 'I've always meant to ask . . . Is it hard, working at the hospice with people who are . . . well, who might not make it?'

Her mum began to help her put the cakes into the big Tupperware box, glancing at her for a moment before returning to their task. 'It can be difficult, love, yes. But it's also giving the people – and their families – a chance for a bit of relief and support.' Angel could feel her mum's eyes on her again as she concentrated on putting the cakes in the box. 'And you have to remember, not everyone is there because they're reaching the end. Some people are there for palliative care, and to help us readjust their medications, to help with short-term health issues . . . all sorts of things. You just have to be understanding, you know?'

Angel nodded, and her mum smiled at her. 'I already know you are – and you're going to be an amazing doctor!' She licked a stray bit of icing off her finger as they finished packing up the snacks. 'You're not a bad baker, either!'

As she finished gathering the stuff together to take to school, Angel felt her mother still lingering around her, seeming a little bit anxious. Both her hands were cupped around her mug of tea, and she had the air of someone waiting for the right time to say something, pacing around the small living room, distractedly half-watching the breakfast news on the TV murmuring away in the background, then looking back to Angel.

'Mum, you're hovering more than a UFO. It's doing my head in. What's up?'

Her mum genuinely seemed surprised that her daughter had noticed, but she set down her mug on the TV table and drew in a breath. Angel noticed that Ruth's nerves seemed tinged with . . . excitement? Angel stopped putting stuff in her bag to turn her full attention to her mum.

'I . . . I have a date tomorrow night. With Victor. He's just asked me,' Ruth said slowly, then bit her lip as if waiting for Angel's reaction. She was glad that her instinct was to smile, because she could see her mum's shoulders visibly relax with relief.

'That's great, Mum,' Angel said, even as an unwelcome tinge of actual *jealousy* (mortifying), and some other, far more complicated feelings about her dad began to gnaw gently at her insides. 'Err, where's he taking you?' She paused, suddenly realising – this could be her chance to vet This Victor. 'Is he coming here to pick you up? What time?' *OK, bit obvious.*

'I'm not sure, he said a nice restaurant. He'll be here seven-ish I think, and . . . My goodness.' Her mum flopped on to the sofa, the tails of her dressing gown belt flipping into the air. 'I haven't been on a date in years, darling! What do I say? What do I *wear*?'

Angel glanced at her phone, and saw both that time was pressing on, and also a message from Izzy saying she was about to get to the corner they usually met on. But, tricky and emotional and weird as it was, her mum needed a pep talk and that was more important for now. Angel sat down on the edge of the sofa beside her.

'You've already chatted loads to – ' she had to stop herself from adding 'this' – 'Victor, right? You know you've got plenty to talk about, so that shouldn't be an issue. And worst case, just talk about me!' she added with a chuckle. 'Or . . . his kids?' Angel was fishing, but she reckoned she might as well.

'We do talk about our kids. You, his grown-up son and daughter . . .'

Hmm. Great. 'Well, there you go. And in terms of what to wear?' Angel paused, thinking through her mum's wardrobe. 'It's Christmas, so . . . what about that green dress you wore to Aunty Helen's wedding? It's festive, and looks amazing on you, maybe with the gold necklace I got you for your birthday?'

Her mum's eyes lit up. 'You're right, that could work. Thank you, my Angel pie!' She paused. 'I'm so glad you're OK with all this.'

Angel nodded, even if she felt that little bit of *not*-OK-with-all-this. She sprang up and bent down to kiss her mum on the cheek. 'No problem. Call me fairy ... god-daughter? OK don't, that sounds weird. Either way, it'll all be fine, I'm sure. Now, I'd better get to school. See you later, Mum! We can sort out your accessory options for tomorrow!'

And, Angel thought, *start preparing to assess This Victor . . .*

Twenty minutes later, still thinking about her mum's new romantic life with a mix of emotions and not a little bit of trepidation, Angel began the long struggle in to school carrying all the cakes and snacks. Izzy met her on the corner, and grudgingly offered to carry the – much lighter – packages of popcorn. Angel remembered the message she'd revealed this morning on the advent calendar.

Wish for something and believe it might come true!

She would have wished for a car to take them to school today, but it was still months until she could even get her *provisional* licence, and then there was no way she or her mum could actually afford a car. At least walking was a good workout, she supposed. Barely able to see over the top of the boxes of cakes, Angel was struggling to both hold them and to keep up with the detailed plot breakdown that Izzy was giving about her favourite 'reality' TV show. But then she heard footsteps jogging up behind them.

'That's an awfully big packed lunch.' Caspar moved around and stopped in front of her, forcing Angel to come to a halt.

'Har har,' Angel said, moving to step around him, but he still blocked their way.

'Need a hand?' He gave a half smile, and Izzy made no hesitation in proffering her bag filled with the packages of popcorn with a grateful sigh.

Caspar laughed as he slung it over his shoulder, then nodded at Angel.

'I'm fi—' she began, but he deftly lifted the boxes from her arms with a knowing smirk. Angel felt an odd fizz go through her at the effortlessness of the move, in spite of herself. He began easily ambling along with the burden as they started towards school.

'Cheers, Casper,' Izzy said, raising an eyebrow at Angel, which she studiously ignored.

'No worries. Are these all for the screening later?' he said.

Angel nodded. 'Yup. We'll sort out a concession stand beforehand. You'll be all ready to go with the projection, right?'

'Yeah, course. And I was thinking, maybe we could do a quiz after the film? I started jotting down a few questions last night. Could charge a little bit of extra money to enter that, too?'

Angel had to admit that was actually a pretty good idea. 'Yeah, that should work.'

'Cool. You'll have to sit it out though, I think

 106

you'd have an unfair advantage . . .' He winked at her, and Angel smiled back before she could even think about it. OK, this was getting weird. Since when was Caspar actually friendly towards her? She was glad when they reached the gates of the school, and went to drop the food off in the assembly hall until the film screening later. Angel was starting to feel a nervous excitement about the fundraiser, and by the time lunch came around, a queue was forming at the ticket sales table in the canteen before she had even got there to help.

Sanj and Josh were already there, laughing and joking with each other as they took students' money, tore off tickets and wrote down names.

'Wow, this is looking good,' Angel said, dumping her bag and making her way behind the table. She had to admit she'd half-hoped that for once Caspar would have stepped up and helped out with some of this, especially given Josh was giving up his lunch break to help, but he was nowhere to be seen. She didn't want to seem too bitter, so she avoided asking Josh where his best friend had got to. The queue got bigger, and Angel was pleased when just twenty minutes later they had to announce that the screening was sold out.

She noticed Josh typing away on his phone as they tidied up the table, and couldn't help spotting Caspar's name flash up in the reply on the screen as he put it down on the table. Josh frowned as he picked it up again to read it, but Angel told herself to stop being nosy. Still, she did also have a brainwave for Josh's next Secret Santa gift – a phone case. His current one was scruffy, to say the least! She ignored the Caspar question. Things were looking up! And as she went over to help count the cash, they were looking better still. It seemed some of her fellow students had even donated a bit extra over the ticket price. The fundraiser was going to be great!

Except . . .

Fifteen minutes before the 4pm start time, the hall was filling up with excited students, the air with Christmas music, and people were happily tucking into the snacks that Angel had made. They had almost sold all the popcorn and cakes. It all seemed to be going amazingly.

Except!

Caspar *blinking* Johnson – keeper of the film on his laptop, flakiest of all flakey boys – was still nowhere to be seen!

'Where *is* he?' Angel bit out between gritted teeth, then faking a smile at Yasmin Shahidi, selling her the last packet of popcorn. 'It's meant to start soon. People are going to kick off!'

Josh was starting to look pretty stressed out – and it didn't help when Tilda came storming over, hands on her hips. 'Those audio visual boys are giving me shrugs, Angel. Where is the film? We need to set up!'

Angel thought back to her calendar's challenge that morning, about believing a wish might come true. She wished with every fibre of her being that Caspar would show up right this very second, or some kind of miracle would save this screening from turning from *amazing* to *disastrous*.

Josh startled as his phone screen lit up with a

call, and he rushed away from Tilda and Angel to answer it. A short while later, he rushed back. 'OK, I'm going to go and meet Caspar to grab his laptop. His dad's driven him over in the car. He's really sorry. I . . . I'll be back in a sec.'

His dad? Angel felt her emotions run from angry and irritated to sort of concerned. She knew Caspar was bad at time-keeping, but this seemed like something different. She had to stop herself from pulling out her phone and texting him herself. At least they'd have the film to project soon. Telling herself, once again, to mind her own business, she focussed on selling the last of the cupcakes, and crossing her fingers that the kids in the school hall didn't get too restless while they finished setting everything up.

As the lights in the assembly hall finally dimmed and the famous airport scene of the movie began to unfold, Angel sighed with relief. Maybe her wish had come true after all! She supposed there wouldn't be a quiz about the film afterwards if Caspar wasn't there to do it, but perhaps they could do one for the next screening.

But even with the situation rescued, she couldn't help wonder – what could possibly be going on to mean Caspar would miss their first fundraiser?

♥ lll ♥

CHAPTER 9

Saturday 6th December

'How's it looking?' Angel asked, balancing on a stool to try and place some of the decorations nearer the top of the Christmas tree in the living room the next day. It was the same every year: the artificial – but very convincing – tree was really too big for the small space, but it made both Angel and her mum happy, so they kept it. Plus, why waste the money on a new one?

'A bit more to the left?' her mum said, cocking her head to one side with her hands on her hips. '*Your* left,' she added with a chuckle.

Angel huffed some air over her bottom lip at all

the exertion. 'OK, that'll have to do,' she said. 'Oh, pass me the star?'

But Ruth was back rummaging through a different box of spangly things – her jewellery box. 'What do you think of these earrings?' she asked Angel.

'I think you should be keeping an eye on me. I don't want to fall off this thing and break my neck. Imagine the guilt!' Her mum laughed, and Angel gave a weary smile. 'Yes, by the way. Those will go really well. Now, how about you pass me the star?'

'All right, keep your knickers on,' her mum said. 'Worst case, we can plonk *you* at the top of the tree, can't we, *Angel*?' Ruth laughed heartily at her own joke, and Angel, of course, rolled her eyes, even though she couldn't help a chuckle herself. Placing the ornament at the tree's pinnacle at last, she climbed off the stool gratefully and then went over to the plug.

'OK, hit the lights,' she said to her mum, who flicked off the switch in the living room. This was always the best part! Angel turned on the plug at the wall, and they both looked towards the Christmas tree, ready to gaze at the illumination in awe. But . . . nothing.

'Oh dear, one of the fairy lights must be fused,' her mum said, heading over to carefully begin unwinding the string from the tree once Angel had unplugged them. 'We should have checked before we put them on.'

'Yeah.' Angel sighed. She helped her mum unwind the lights, but the thought of trying to figure out which bulb was fused was too much. The string of lights was too old to keep anyway. She was pretty sure the . . . what are they called, fairy light engineers? . . . of today had figured out a way around this problem. These were probably more hand-downs from her grandmother, just like most of their electrical equipment. 'You know what, Mum?' Angel said. 'You go and start getting ready for your date. I'm going to pop into town before the shops shut and buy a new set of lights. We're going to finish this tree today!'

Her mum smiled gratefully and Angel shrugged on her coat and wound her scarf around her neck, ready to embrace the chill as she walked to the high street. Maybe it was from decorating the Christmas tree, or the light sprinkling of snowflakes beginning to drift down from the sky as dusk approached, but Angel was feeling rather festive! She even remembered the – rather specific – message on her advent calendar that morning:

Buy someone a coffee.

Karl at the Crafty Cuppa had actually introduced a scheme recently where you could buy a coffee on credit, essentially so that someone less fortunate could come in and get one for free. Maybe that was what the calendar meant? After all, her Secret Santa was someone local . . .

Either way, Angel decided she had enough time before the hardware shop closed to pop in to the café, buy herself a hot chocolate, and fulfil her calendar's challenge, too. The place was busy as

Angel queued up, and through the window she could see that the ice rink was also now open, and heaving with eager skaters. She couldn't wait to find a moment to go herself. Izzy usually took a bit of persuading to strap on the blades, but Ola was always up for it, and Angel was pretty sure between them they could convince Izz!

Buzzing with her little good deed after she had paid both for her own drink and put credit on for someone else's, Angel blew through the little sip hole in the lid to her hot chocolate and headed down to the concourse to watch the skaters for a moment on her way to the hardware shop. Through the crowd as she looked across the rink, she could have sworn she saw a familiar figure in a duffle coat. Caspar 'very much the ghost' Johnson. Angel really wanted to go over and ask him about his disappearing act at their first film screening. She hoped there wasn't anything wrong. But as she glanced at the time on her phone, she saw it was heading towards six o'clock. She'd better stick to her task and go to get the lights for the tree – *but,* she thought to herself, *if Caspar was still hanging out at the rink after she was done, he'd better get ready for some serious explaining!*

The array of different kinds of fairy lights in the shop was a bit overwhelming, but Angel chose some simple twinkling white ones – which were, crucially, within her budget. As she was paying, she noticed Sanj and his brother in the queue in front of her, and greeted her classmate with a smile.

'Angel, hey,' Sanj said. 'This is my brother, Manny.' Angel smiled at them both. She had to admit, Manny really was a good-looking guy. He flashed a smile at her in return, then turned around to the cashier to pay for the cans of paint they were carrying. 'My dad's roped us in to helping paint the bathroom,' Sanj explained, pulling a face. 'It's not exactly my forte, but Manny here is pretty handy with the DIY. I suppose that's why he's studying to be an engineer!'

'Not even remotely a related thing,' Manny said over his shoulder with a chuckle as he finished paying. Angel already knew that she'd be required to report back on every stage of this interaction to Izzy, who would no doubt be very angry not to have been tagging along on this errand, so she made lots of mental notes – and then she thought of something. 'Hey, Sanj, were you hanging out with Caspar and Josh and that lot earlier? I thought I saw Caspar at the ice rink, and I wondered if he was going to be there for a while? I want to find out from my so-called partner on our little two-person fundraising committee exactly what happened last night.'

Sanj shook his head. 'Nah, don't know, I wasn't with them. I think I'll be seeing Josh later, though. There's a screening of a horror film we're both really into – *Scum Night 3* – at the cinema tonight. Not exactly the festive fare we're working with for the screenings at school!' He laughed, and Angel joined in. 'But I did see Caspar with a girl a bit earlier.'

Angel froze. She couldn't help it. Caspar was with a *girl*? Was that why he had skipped out on them after school on Friday? Who was she? Her heart sank, then it sank even further at the very fact she felt upset at the idea of him dating someone. 'Oh right,' she managed. 'Anyway, see you later.' She waved goodbye to Sanj and Manny as they headed out of the store, and paid for the Christmas tree lights, her festive feelings from earlier truly – and kind of embarrassingly – dampened.

'Was that the door? Oh gosh, why am I so nervous? Angel, sweetheart, can you answer it? I'll be down in a minute.'

Angel never *had* seen her mum look so nervous – or gorgeous! She told her as much, trying to will away her own feelings of awkwardness about what this whole 'mum dating' thing might mean for their future as a family. Not to mention the weirdness about the dad-shaped hole This Victor might be thinking he could fill, which he definitely never could ... Oh, and then there was the jealousy, especially as the whole romantic escapade was making her think about the other thing she really didn't want to confront – Caspar Johnson having a girlfriend. *Ugh. Why does it matter?*

Angel half-hoped that it would be Izzy at the door, but it was very unlikely she'd be an hour early. Her friend was due to come over later, and they were planning to order takeaway and stream a load of films and TV shows while eating too much. But first Angel had some assessing to do.

She pulled open the door, eyebrow already arched.

'Hi there,' the man at the door said. 'You must be Angel? Fitting name!'

Angel pursed her lips. This Victor was off to a bad start, as far as she was concerned. Trying too hard. But she had to admit he had a friendly smile, and a lightly greying moustache balanced on top of it made him seem quite approachable. He wore dark trousers, a long brown overcoat, and had a silky scarf draped around his neck. There was a warm, spicy smell about him that seemed to suggest he'd got suited and booted especially for the date.

'Nice to meet you,' she said sceptically, stepping aside. Victor whipped off the flat woollen cap he was wearing, and Angel eyed his slightly balding brown head surrounded by thinning afro hair. He proffered a bunch of flowers towards her, and she noticed he had another bunch clutched under his arm.

'These ones are for you,' he said, and Angel noticed his hand was trembling a little as he held them out to her. Was *he* nervous? Was this kind of . . . cute? He smiled again, his eyes crinkling warmly. Maybe she was being too harsh on him. So far he actually seemed quite sweet. It was just hard to picture anyone being good enough for her mum.

'Thanks, Victor,' Angel said, 'Nice move.' He looked a bit hurt, so she rephrased. 'I mean, that's really nice of you.' She took the flowers, guessing that she shouldn't offer to put the others in a vase, too, as he'd want to give them to her mum himself first. He edged towards her as she ran water into the glass vase by the sink, unwrapped her flowers and plopped them inside. She took a deep breath, realising she probably didn't have much time until her mum came down the stairs for interrogation. But as she opened her mouth, planning to issue some kind of subtle (or not-so-subtle) warning, Victor beat her to it.

'Err, listen, Angel ... I understand this is probably a bit awkward for you, and I can't claim to know what it might be like to see your mum dating again. But I'm going to do my best to show Ruth a lovely time tonight, and we can see what happens from there, eh?'

Angel folded her arms, and raised *both* her eyebrows at that. She almost laughed at how flustered Victor got at her non-verbal response.

'I ... uh ... I meant nothing suggestive by that. I mean just in terms of ... I meant if she might want to go on another date, or maybe—'

Angel held up a hand, smiling. 'Relax, Victor. That's really good to know. I'm not going to lie, if you hurt my mum, you're going to have me to deal with. But I really hope you guys have a lovely time. She'll be down any second.' Angel saw a shadow cast down the stairs. 'In fact, there she is now,' she said with a smile, watching as Victor turned and her mother descended the staircase with a wiggle in her walk that Angel had definitely never seen before.

'Wow,' Victor said, as Ruth smiled and did a twirl. The two older lovebirds cooed at one another as Victor helped Ruth into her coat. Angel felt a weird mixture of grossed-out, sad-ish, really happy, and . . . yeah, she hated to admit it, but still kind of jealous. Just as Angel waved them goodbye, she saw Izzy making her way up the short path to their house. What do you know, she was a bit early for once. Izzy jerked her glove-covered thumb over her shoulder as she headed towards Angel's front door.

'Hello? Score one for Ruth, he was a handsome devil!' Izzy said as she strode through the door Angel held open. 'Well, like, for an old-timer.'

'If you say so,' Angel muttered, closing the front door and doing a full body shiver at the thought of . . . all of that. Izzy shrugged out of her coat, and pulled a pretend-sad face at Angel.

'Believe me, if anyone can relate to the weirdness of parents finding new relationships, it's me, Ange. But Ruth is never going to bring anyone into your life that will throw what you guys have out of whack,' she said, striding over and gripping Angel's shoulders. Angel gave her friend a weak smile, and Izzy returned it more forcefully.

'Yeah, I suppose you're right,' Angel said, and Izzy released her, striding away to collapse onto the sofa and peruse the take-away menus Angel had left out.

'Unlike my dad, and his delusional thoughts about me and my stepmonster having some crazy bonding-session next weekend,' Izzy said. 'He wants us to go on a day-trip to London. Can you think of anything more hellish?'

Angel chuckled, settling on to the sofa beside her friend. 'I can, actually.' She'd *love* to go to

London for the day – even though they were just over an hour away from the capital, she rarely got to go there. Museums, concerts, shopping ... What wasn't to like? It was one of her favourite things to daydream about. Now it was her turn to pull a mock-frown at Izzy.

'It'll be fine, Izz. Try to keep an open mind.'

Izzy huffed. 'Easier said than done. Anyway, enough of all that, let's get some food in, I'm starving!'

They ordered, and half-watched the screen as they chomped on spring rolls and pad thai. Angel thought she might have to do the Heimlich on Izzy when she got around to recounting how she had run into Sanj and Manny at the shop earlier. After going over the interaction in forensic detail for the third time, Angel said, 'I'm beginning to wish I'd just filmed the whole thing on my phone!'

'Ooh, maybe you should next time,' Izzy said with absolutely no hint of irony. 'No, forget it, actually – next time I'm going to be there. I'm going to *live* at that DIY shop from now on. He's bound to go back there if he loves getting his hands dirty, right?' Her expression went all dreamy, and Angel nudged her friend in the ribs as the streaming service counted them down into the fifth episode of the series they were watching.

After staring at the screen for a while, Angel looked over at Izzy with a sidelong glance, and drew a breath, trying to sound nonchalant. 'Hey, so had *you* heard anything about Caspar having a new girlfriend?'

Izzy concentrated on the TV, but Angel could see the knowing half-smile on her face. 'No, I haven't heard anything like that,' she said. 'Why?'

'No reason.' Angel reached for the last spring roll and chewed it thoughtfully. This was weird. She realised that for the first time maybe ever, she might actually have to admit she had a crush on someone.

She just couldn't quite believe who it was.

CHAPTER 10

Sunday 7th December

Angel was already at the kitchen table with her textbooks spread out in front of her, munching toast, when her mum ambled downstairs in her dressing gown yawning the next morning. Last night, Izzy was calling a taxi to take her home by the time Ruth had put a key in the door and floated in on cloud nine. The date with Victor had clearly gone really well.

'Oh, morning, sweetheart,' Ruth said now. 'Do you know, I actually had a *dream* about the lobster ravioli Victor and I ate at the restaurant last night!' Her mum's eyes fell on the open loaf of bread on the table and she grimaced, while Angel chuckled.

'Crashing back to reality, eh?' she said, and Ruth reached over to try and tickle her before plonking a couple of slices into the toaster for her own breakfast. 'I'm glad you had fun,' Angel added.

'I did, thanks, sweetheart.' Her mum looked over at their slightly dilapidated Christmas tree, now at least illuminated nicely in the corner of their living room. 'Hey, maybe we should check out the festive market in town today,' she said. 'Later on, I mean, once you've had a chance to get a few more facts and figures crammed into that brain of yours?'

Angel smiled over at her mum. She did appreciate how much Ruth understood and supported her studying, but she also remembered that according to her calendar, her challenge today was:

Get in touch with nature.

OK so it wasn't exactly trees and bees and flowers, but a trip to the town's winter fair would be getting out and about a bit at least. She could start thinking about some Christmas presents, and there was a strong likelihood of some tasty treats to eat on those stalls, too.

'Yeah, sounds good. Give me an hour or two and we can head out!' Angel said, as her mum put her plate of toast down and munched on a corner of it wistfully, still clearly thinking about her fancy pasta from last night.

A couple of hours later, Angel and her mum were wrapped up warm and heading down the high street, soaking up the bustling atmosphere even as the biting wind whipped around them. The Christmas fair was in the square off to the side of the Bluebell Hospice, and a local brass band had set up at one corner, playing 'It's Beginning to Look a Lot Like Christmas'. Angel couldn't argue there! The smell of cinnamon and baked goods swirled around them, and people browsed the little stalls selling handcrafted ornaments and fun Christmas gift ideas. In fact, Angel spotted a table full of phone cases, and took her mum's elbow to drag her over to it. Secret Santa gift number two sorted! Angel selected one that was in the colours of Josh's favourite football team, having finally got a good look at his badges, and handed it to the young man running the stall to pay.

'Interesting choice,' her mum remarked. 'Going to be heading out on the terraces any time soon?'

Angel laughed. 'It's for Josh Yorke.'

'Oh?' Her mum perked up, and Angel definitely needed her to perk down again. Not everyone could be all loved up!

'Nope, it's nothing like that. I'm his Secret Santa, at school.'

'Ahhh,' Ruth said, sounding only slightly disappointed. 'Well you'd better squirrel that away pretty quickly. There's Josh now, over there with Caspar. Why don't we go and say hello?'

Angel's heart both fluttered and sank as she looked over to where her mum was pointing. Up on a grassy verge nearby there were stacks of real Christmas trees ready to be sold, alongside a netting machine. It looked like Josh and Caspar had volunteered to man the stall. The trees were sold every year as one of the school's fundraising drives. Angel's mum was never too keen on getting a live tree, with their dropping needles and the depressing sight of the browning tree sitting on the kerb come January. But Angel also suspected it was because they were quite expensive, even if the money was going to a good place. Her mum gave a lot to the hospice every day already. Either way, Angel was less than thrilled now as her mum started striding off in the direction of the tree stall. Stuffing Josh's gift into her bag, she reluctantly followed on behind her, and as they reached the stall where the boys were selling the trees, Angel was relieved that Caspar was occupied by hoisting one of them into the netting machine.

'Hello, Joshua,' her mum said, 'Well done for helping out here today. Sell, sell, sell, eh?'

Josh laughed. 'We're trying, Mrs Green! I think it's going pretty well so far. Hey, Angel,' he added, smiling, and Angel said a quick hello back. Her eyes strayed back over to Caspar, and then she noticed who he was helping. Tilda Chase – who was actually *laughing*, which seemed to be the result of Caspar's quips as he pulled the tree he'd been netting out of the machine. Then the normally-staid Tilda actually leaned over and touched his arm, her eyes locked on his. She gestured over to the car park, then batted her eyes at Caspar, who hoisted the tree easily onto one shoulder and winked at her. *Ugh*.

Had Angel been blind to this the whole time? Tilda and Caspar were engaging in some serious flirtation. Maybe she was even the girl Sanj had seen Caspar with the other day? With a woolly hat covering her hair and a scarf wrapped around her neck, Tilda might not have been easy for Sanj to recognise from distance. Especially if she had looked, like she did now, as though she was actually enjoying herself for once ... Angel stared at their retreating backs as Caspar and Tilda walked off with the Christmas tree.

'Angel?'

'Hmm?' She turned back to her mum suddenly, feeling herself heat inside her coat. Had she been busted shooting eye-daggers at their school's newest power couple? OK maybe she was getting ahead of herself, but it made sense.

'I was just saying to Josh how great it is that you're all getting behind the hospice this year for the fundraiser. We really do appreciate it!'

Angel was hoping to leave the stall before Caspar came back, but her mum got distracted chatting to Josh and his mum, who had come over briefly to collect her own tree. Before she could escape, she saw Caspar jogging back over to the stall, the early-afternoon sunshine making his brown afro glow around his head, and his eyes twinkle, and— *Ugh, get a grip, Angel! Think about what you just saw, and get real.*

Then mortification descended as Caspar looked right in her direction, catching her staring. *Great!* As he came over, Angel was a little surprised that Caspar went straight in for a hug with her mum.

'Hi, Ruth,' he said as she gave him a little squeeze, then they both seemed to back away from one another quickly. 'Err, long time no see,' Caspar added quickly, and Angel's mum nodded.

'Right. Yes, good to see you again. Uh . . . How are your parents keeping?'

'Good, good,' Caspar replied.

OK, this is weird, Angel thought. Though, of course, it was only a few years ago that their families used to hang out all the time. She shouldn't be surprised that Caspar could turn on the charm for her mum. 'Hi Caspar,' she said pointedly, and he turned to her, his expression a bit sheepish now.

'Angel, hey. I meant to drop you a message, erm, about the other day . . .'

Angel waved a gloved hand in the air dismissively, even though inside she was dying to hear his excuse. And apology. And kind of just keen to have Caspar talk to her at all. He seemed about to explain further, but then he was momentarily called away by a customer asking about prices. Angel's mum spotted one of her colleagues heading over to the hot chocolate stand.

'I'm just going to pop over and say hello to Tamia, sweetheart. Why don't I grab us a couple of hot chocolates, too? You can stay here for a moment with your friends.'

'Oh that's OK, I—' Angel began, but Ruth had already jogged over and began laughing animatedly with her workmate. She vaguely heard the name *Victor* mentioned, and decided she could definitely sit out hearing her mum coo over her date last night. She pulled out her phone and freed a solitary thumb from her glove out into the cold to text Izzy. But just as she did, a shadow fell across her screen, and she looked up to see Caspar looking down at her earnestly again.

'Sorry about that. It's busy today. I, um, I really wanted to apologise for missing the screening on Friday.'

Angel found herself looking up into Caspar's eyes, his brows knitted together in an unusually pained expression, and she had to confess that she believed him. And that up this close she could see that his eyes were actually a really unusual kind of dark-honey colour that she'd never really thought about before. And she was still staring. And still silent . . .

She cleared her throat. 'Yeah, I mean it would

have been nice for you to drop me a message or something,' she said, though she struggled to keep any authority in her voice under his melting stare. Is that how he looked at Tilda? *As if*. Angel desperately tried to shake the thought, and glanced away, flushed and feeling even more irritated despite knowing it was a bit unreasonable. 'It was actually not cool to do that, Caspar. How do you think I felt, given that we were *supposed* to have been working on it together? You just didn't show up and left me looking like a . . . a mug.'

She almost jumped as she felt his hand reach out to rest on her shoulder. Even through his fingerless gloves, and her coat, and jumper, and the T-shirt underneath, she could feel the warmth of his hand.

'I really want to explain,' Caspar said, his voice low. His eyes drifted to where his hand sat on her shoulder and he seemed to remember that his usual charm probably wouldn't work on her. Angel wasn't so sure actually, but he lifted it away, and shoved both of his hands into his pockets. 'Sometime I will, but you have to trust me, I would never abandon you without a good reason.' Angel didn't know what to say. A half-smile crept onto Caspar's face. 'I definitely wouldn't want you looking like a *mug*.'

Angel couldn't help smiling too. *Ugh*. To be fair, maybe she'd been watching too many East End gangster films. They both turned as they heard Josh calling Caspar's name and gesticulating at the queue of people all waiting to get their trees.

'You'd better go,' Angel said, but Caspar didn't seem in a hurry to move off as he continued looking down at her. She bit her lip, and Josh shouted Caspar's name again.

'There in a sec, mate,' Caspar called over his shoulder, then turned back to her. 'Next time I promise I won't let you down, AG.' He winked, and with his deep voice still ringing in her ears, Angel watched Caspar Johnson turn and jog away.

Don't get sucked in, Angel told herself. But it was probably too late already . . .

Angel and her mum got home, looking forward to warming up and enjoying the Christmas cookies they'd bought at one of the stalls. But they were greeted with a distinctly *chilly* welcome as they came in through the front door.

'Could have sworn I put the timer on,' Ruth said. She walked through to the kitchen and opened the cupboard where their old, dilapidated boiler was housed. Angel had a feeling she knew what the issue was. Bessie the boiler had surely, and finally, given up the ghost. Alarmed as she heard her mum start to bash it in her time-honoured method of trying to get things to work, Angel made her way over and put her hands on her hips.

'She's had her day, Mum. We're going to have to get a new one.'

They both looked at one another, because they knew what that meant – a lot of money. And at Christmas, too. Angel saw the concern in her mum's big brown eyes, and wished she was already a doctor earning enough money to easily pay for fixing things like this. Her mum made their lives work so comfortably, even when it was hard, and without any complaints. Angel never wanted for anything. And yet she knew that things other people might take for granted – like paying for insurance to cover the boiler if it broke down – were outside her mum's financial scope.

'Don't worry, Mum. Maybe old Bessie here can just about make it through another winter if we can get her fixed? If not, we'll make it work. I promise I'll help. And in the meantime that's why we've got coats, eh?'

Her mum did manage to raise a smile at that, even though Angel could still tell she was definitely worried. 'It'll be all right, darling, yes. I'll make us some tea. At least it was a nice day up until all of this, eh?'

Angel only *kind of* agreed with that, thinking again about her interaction with Caspar, and his flirting with Tilda.

'And I know you said you're just his Secret Santa,' her mum continued, and Angel's eyes narrowed suspiciously, 'but if you ask me, that Josh has grown into quite a lovely young man. You guys are organising a school disco for the end of the year, aren't you? If you were thinking you might want a date for that, I reckon you could do worse than him . . .'

Angel cringed at the thought as she watched her mum dunk the teabags in the hot water she'd just poured out, already feeling a bit warmer despite the heating issues. At least Ruth wasn't asking about Caspar. *That* might well be a lot closer to home. Angel actually wanted to ask about the weirdly friendly greeting he and her mum had shared, too, but she figured it was best to keep Ruth away from any inklings about her interest in Caspar. Besides, for now they had bigger, more boiler-shaped issues to deal with.

Angel was beginning to think a Christmas miracle wouldn't go amiss right about now . . .

CHAPTER 11

Monday 8th December

Monday morning came around quicker than Angel had anticipated as she'd shivered in her bed the night before – but she woke up toasty warm. *Huh?* Confused, especially when she heard lots of banging and clattering downstairs, Angel rolled out from under her duvet, made her way downstairs . . .

And let out a yelp!

A broad-shouldered figure was standing in their kitchen with his back to her, screwing the cover back on to the boiler. Angel indignantly and emphatically tied her dressing gown's belt, and after managing to swallow her heart back into its appropriate place, cleared her throat. The man turned around – and she saw the slightly wary smile of Victor, shirtsleeves rolled.

'Err, hi. Where's my mum?' Angel asked, only vaguely aware of sounding a bit rude, but then she heard footsteps coming down the stairs.

'Here it is!' her mum called, waving what looked like a screwdriver over her head.

'Oh, not to worry, Ruthie love, I found mine in the end. Thank you though!' Victor said, still shooting wary glances Angel's way.

'Ah, morning Ange!' her mum said cheerily.

Love? Angel was still hearing that way-too-early term of affection to her mum from Victor echoing in her head. She suppressed a groan and folded her arms as Ruth dotted a kiss onto Angel's cheek then headed over to Victor.

'So I was messaging Vic, as usual, from the Artic tundra that was my bed last night,' Ruth was saying – not really an image Angel needed before her first cup of tea – 'and lo and behold, he told

 142

me that he used to be a boiler mechanic back in the day! What are the odds? We learn something new about each other every day, eh?'

Angel nodded, and fought even more valiantly to keep her face from completely screwing up as her mum went on tiptoes to plant a smacker on Victor's lips. 'He wanted to come over right then and there, but I said not to, didn't want to wake you. But crack of dawn this morning, there he was at our door!'

Angel had to admit that it *was* pretty sweet of him. Clearly he was seriously into her mum! 'Thanks, Victor,' she said, walking into the kitchen to give him an only faintly grudging but also sincere smile. 'That's really nice of you to help us out. Quite the multi-talented guy, then?'

Victor already had a thin sheen of sweat from labouring over the boiler, but his flush deepened a bit on his shining brown skin at that. 'Oh, dear, don't know about all that. But it was honestly no problem at all, Angel. Really glad I could help. It's a temporary fix, you know, but it should tide you both over until the New Year, hopefully . . .'

Humble too, eh? The cynic in her wanted to be, well, cynical – but This Victor actually was quite a sweetheart, Angel realised. And it was a huge relief to have the boiler sorted. Her grin at him widened, and she could just feel the beams of pleasure coming off her mum as she watched the scene. She still felt a bit weird about the whole situation and how Victor was meant to fit into their lives, but she couldn't deny he'd been exactly what they needed today. Tomorrow, though, and the next day . . .?

'Tea?' Ruth said brightly, interrupting Angel's thoughts, but she excused herself to head to the – thankfully now-hot – shower and get ready for school. The day was already off to a fairly good start, and as she scratched off the wax on the next day of her advent calendar, Angel felt pretty confident that she'd already *done* the challenge it was extending today:

Pay someone a compliment.

She was fairly sure she'd made Victor's morning with one!

But as she met Izzy on the corner, she reckoned she could spare one more compliment, just to be certain. 'You're looking really ...' She scanned her friend and especially the extra-rolled-up grey pleated school skirt she had on. 'Actually what *is* happening with this situation, Izz?' Angel said, gesturing at it. 'It's four degrees this morning. Aren't you freezing?'

'I've decided my legs are my best feature,' Izzy said breezily (or was it her teeth chattering) as she linked arms with Angel. She kicked one leg in the air in front of them as they walked, like a can-can dancer.

'I'm not looking to join the Moulin Rouge, hon,' Angel said, then smirked. 'So ... planning an after-school trip to the DIY store, are you?'

Izzy stuck her tongue out at Angel, but chuckled a little. 'Actually, looking good is just for me, but it won't *hurt* if we do run into a certain smoking-hot older brother at some point, too.'

Angel had big plans for a fresh start at the school council meeting that morning. She strolled into the room, even carrying a bag of the mini doughnuts that were like gold dust to actually get hold of at the Crafty Cuppa, having stopped in there with Izzy before they got to school. As her fellow students began to trickle in to their meeting room, she enjoyed watching their eyes light up with glee as she offered them round.

Sanj sauntered in with Josh, both talking about something that Angel could only assume was that nasty sounding horror film Sanj had mentioned when she ran into him. She remembered the other bit of information he'd mentioned, but chose to completely push out of her mind the notion of being jealous at Caspar maybe having a girlfriend – and it maybe being Tilda Chase – at least for now. It *was* a bit odd how much time Sanj and Josh seemed to be spending together, though. The gossip in Angel (and OK, the jealous girl with the crush) wondered if it was maybe as a result of Josh's best mate being otherwise occupied . . .

Tilda and Oliva, who had been conferring in the corner as the rest of them arrived, made their way over to the main table they'd congregated around. Angel tried not to narrow her eyes at the willowy brunette council head.

'Ooh,' Olivia said, noticing the doughnuts, but just as Angel was about to offer her the last one, Tilda's hand swooped down. Angel slid the bag away back towards Olivia before she could even think about it. Ignoring Tilda's indignant stare, Angel gave the blonde girl a smile and wink, and Olivia seemed grateful at the acknowledgement. But she straightened up as the head of the council called the meeting to order.

'I'm on a diet anyway,' Tilda muttered, before saying, 'OK, everyone. Let's get down to business.' She scanned the council with a disappointed look on her face and a slight shake of her head. Angel looked around the table and had a feeling she knew why. 'Now,' Tilda continued, glancing down at the inevitable agenda Olivia had passed around. 'We'll get to the school disco planning in a bit, but before that – I'm very pleased to say that the first film screening fundraiser was a roaring success, so—'

Just as Tilda spoke, once again, Caspar finally tumbled in to the room, looking genuinely flustered. 'Sorry, everyone,' he said straight away, finding an empty seat and sitting in it quickly. 'These early starts are sometimes a bit tough for me.' Angel looked at him – uniform crumpled, his curls uncombed, a slight frown between his brows. He still, of course, looked really handsome, and she had to look away when he flashed his half-smile at Tilda, who seemed to perk up at that . . . But Angel did wonder what could be up with him. She was beginning to get the impression it wasn't just flakiness that was keeping him occupied. Maybe that was wishful thinking, though – he was probably up late messaging flirtily with their faithful council leader for all she knew . . .

'Oh, no problem, Caspar,' Tilda was saying, and even Olivia looked at her with a little surprise that he wasn't being reprimanded.

Caspar glanced around the table with an apologetic air, before meeting Angel's eyes, his usual charming smile fading a bit as though it was taking some effort today. The expression on his face made her try to give him a reassuring smile, but he looked away again, seeming really quite stressed out. It wasn't how she was used to seeing him, and something in Angel melted a tiny bit more. Meanwhile, Tilda was still talking.

'Caspar, maybe you could work with me on the school disco sub-committee and we could put someone else on to the Christmas fundraiser team. Josh, why don't you partner with Angel on the next film screening?'

Josh opened his mouth to protest, and it definitely didn't escape Angel that Caspar and his best friend exchanged furtive glances.

'No!' Angel was surprised that the word had come from her mouth! She sat up straighter in her chair and felt the eyes of the committee turn on her. 'Err, we've already been planning the next screening, and it wouldn't be fair for

Caspar not to get to finish all his hard work on this. And he'd actually let me know it might be tough for him to make the screening on Friday, I should have said.' Angel sort of regretted lying for him, but it almost seemed worth it when she noticed the tiny hint of a smile on his lips as she spoke.

'OK then. Caspar, what's the next film going to be?' Tilda asked, seeming a bit irritated by the interjection, a hand resting on her hip as she glanced at Angel.

'Err, *Die Hard*?' Angel interjected, worried that Caspar wouldn't remember what they'd been brainstorming. His smile widened a little as he looked over at her.

'An eighteen-rated action film is your next festive feature?' Tilda scoffed. 'I don't think so. See, this is why we might want to rethink—'

'Actually, that was only one option – and a good one,' Caspar said. 'I mean, that film is really an underrated Christmas classic.' He gave Angel the subtlest of winks. 'But if that's a bit too risky for you guys, we had also thought the next one could be *Elf*.'

There were chuckles and nods of approval from the gathered committee.

'Yeah,' Angel said, eyes twinkling. 'Actually, Caspar said something about making elf hats for all the ticket holders. It should be a real laugh.'

'I did?' he said, looking at her. 'Err. I mean, yeah, I did. Great. Making a hundred odd elf hats, no sweat. Should be great. Angel said she couldn't wait to help, so—'

'All right, all right,' Tilda said, waving a hand in the air dismissively. '*Elf* it is.' She batted her eyelids at Caspar, and Angel pursed her lips – but then she felt all hot as they sat down and Caspar turned, flashing her the full beam of his smile as he mouthed, *Nice one, thanks*.

Ola let out a sigh as Angel hunched over her friend's phone screen by their lockers after the final bell, zooming and un-zooming the picture on it. 'I don't see it,' Angel confessed, handing the phone back to Ola.

'You're *sure*?' Ola asked, just as Izzy came up to them.

'Sure about what?' she asked, and Angel turned to her.

'Ola's just got those head shots she had taken,' she explained. Ola had decided to get some professional photographs taken in the hope of securing some auditions – there was one of the few UK film studios near their town, and it was her dream to get in front of a director there one day. Angel bugged her eyes in the hopes that Izzy might understand she should be tactful. Fat chance.

'Oh, yeah, these are nice. I mean, shame about that spot, hon. Should have maybe popped a bit of concealer on it?' Izzy said, rubbing Ola's arm sincerely.

Angel turned away from the unfolding scene of awkwardness to open her locker – and was thrilled to see another shiny package inside it. She held up the tag to read it.

All I Want for Christmas . . .
Love, Secret Santa

Angel felt her mouth go a bit dry. One of her favourites – Queen Mariah. She knew the rest of the lyric finished 'is you'. This Secret Santa was really getting quite flirty now! She was almost bursting to know who it might be, and even though they'd all denied it, part of her was still convinced it was just one of her friends, or maybe even that her mum had put them up to it. She looked back over at Ola and Izzy, but they were now engaged in a discussion about airbrushing. She unwrapped the gift, and grinned as she saw Mariah's divalicious face smiling back on a mug.

'Ooh, nice one,' Izzy said, finally breaking away from apologising to Ola for having been so tactless. 'I wish my Secret Santa was decent at picking gifts. Yesterday I got some lavender bath salts that looked like something you'd give your gran . . .'

Angel was beginning to feel the pressure of the whole secret gift exercise – though she had spotted the phone case she had given Josh (having tucked it into his bag earlier) already on his phone, so maybe she was doing something right. But this gift she'd just received felt like more than just a throwaway present from someone lazily participating in the school tradition. All the items she'd received so far seemed as though the person cared, and she was surprised at how good it made her feel. Maybe this anonymous generosity was a good thing! Though Angel couldn't lie – if she could find out who this mystery person was it would be even better.

'Caspar!' She heard a couple of boys shout his name behind her, and turned in the direction of their call to see Caspar striding towards her, carrying armfuls of green paper card. He turned over his shoulder to say, 'Sorry, guys, I'll catch you down at the pitch at six though, yeah?' He turned back towards Angel, finishing, 'Apparently I've got a bit of art and crafts to make a start on.'

His mouth curled into a wry grimace. 'And you'd better be willing to help,' he concluded, coming to a halt in front of Angel. She shrugged and nodded.

'Guess we'll catch up later, Ange?' Izzy said. As she hugged her goodbye, Izzy whispered in her ear, 'Been doing a fair bit of the old *arts and crafts* lately, no?'

Angel pulled a quick face at her, then hugged Ola goodbye, and watched her friends head off. Wordlessly, she followed alongside Caspar as he walked on towards the classroom that was starting to feel quite familiar to Angel. Almost like . . . a sanctuary?

'So,' Caspar said, putting the pile of card down on the central table and making a show of flexing his fingers. 'First of all, thanks for saving my butt in the council meeting this morning – I owe you one. But I thought you should probably be helping out with making these elf hats, seeing as a) you volunteered me, and b) our lino cutting went so well the other day.'

Angel shrugged, but inside she was pleased that

he'd followed through in getting her to help. 'So what you're saying is: I'm both a scholar and an artist?' she said with a grin.

'I suppose so,' Caspar said, eyeing her. 'Much more than I could ever be, anyway. I envy you, to be honest.' He looked away as he spoke, in a way that Angel hadn't really seen him do before, as if he was a bit shy all of a sudden. He always seemed so confident. 'The academic stuff has never really been my strong suit. I feel much more comfortable with art. It . . . it's how I feel most like myself, you know?'

Like himself. Angel had never really thought about it, but she felt the same way when she could think through a maths problem, or write a report for biology. 'I know what you mean,' she said, softly. They had both somehow lowered themselves onto the stools that sat under the table without her really noticing. She turned to him. 'It sounds incredibly geeky to say out loud, but that's how I feel about studying. I get in the zone, and I feel like it helps me understand the world around me a bit more. I . . . I don't always feel like I know how to navigate it. But things like science and medicine help the world make sense to me. *And* it's something I'm actually good at I think, unlike, say, *relaxing*, or expressing myself in some other way, or . . .'

'You've always seemed to express yourself pretty well from what I could see,' Caspar said, looking down to scrape a bit of paint off the table in front of him. Angel was glad he wasn't meeting her eye because she suddenly felt herself start to sweat, conscious of how close they were sitting. But she also felt . . . safe. 'I'm sort of jealous.'

'Jealous? Of *me*?' Angel couldn't help but scoff. 'Caspar the Charmer, with the ultimate gift of the gab?'

He gave a wry half-smile, still directed down at the table. 'Yeah, yeah. But ever since we were kids you seemed to have your path all laid out. Medicine was, like, your chosen future. Me, on the other hand? I had sports, and yeah I guess I've got a bit of charm about me.' He paused and looked over at her with a wink. For once, Angel didn't want to roll her eyes at him. 'But art's what I'm really into. If I'm honest . . .'

'Yeah?'

'Well, I'd love to go to art school. Camberwell, maybe? But that kind of seems like a pipe dream.'

'Why? You're really good. It's definitely not too late to start focussing on that.'

Caspar looked up at her, eyes narrowed sceptically. 'It's not just showing a few paintings and hoping for the best, you know. There's a lot to it. You have to be super-dedicated and even then, who knows if it will work out. I should probably stick to football.'

Angel pursed her lips and shrugged. 'If you're passionate about it, I reckon you can make it happen.'

He made a noncommittal noise and began arranging the sheets of card in front of him. But for some reason, Angel continued, 'And it's being motivated, too. Having someone driving you, who wants you to do well. I think a lot about how if I

make it to becoming a doctor ... Or ... when?'
She saw Caspar nod, like he was about to correct
her himself, and she hid a smile. '*When* I'm a
doctor, I'll finally be able to help out my mum. It's
not just about earning money – I really, really
want to help people too. But Mum does so much
for me, and I know she's really had to struggle to
make ends meet ...'

Caspar looked at her, nodding more
emphatically now. 'I know exactly what you
mean,' he said. 'Family really comes first for me,
too.' For a moment, Angel had a feeling like
Caspar wanted to tell her something more, but
then he straightened up and took a breath.
'Anyway, we should crack on with these hats, eh?
The boys will kill me if I don't turn up for football
practice again.'

Angel raised an eyebrow. 'Again? Good to hear
it's not just me you're standing up. Or um ...' She
regretted the choice of words as soon as they left
her mouth. After all, not turning up at the screening
wasn't just standing *her* up. And who knew what

his arrangements were with Tilda, if they were really an item now. But an odd expression passed across Caspar's face.

'Yeah. Things are ... things are hopefully a bit more stable now though.' He smiled in a gentle way, with a sort of distant look in his eyes that endeared him to Angel even more. It turned into a grin as he looked back at her. 'So, no standing anyone up, down or sideways. *And* more glory on the pitch. It's going to be a good Christmas! Especially if we can make a start on these hats. So, why don't I make one so you can see my vision, and—'

Angel laughed. 'Your vision? Who are you, Philip Treacy?'

'Who?'

She rolled her eyes. 'Google him.'

Still, Angel watched as Caspar's strong fingers quickly manipulated the card into a cone. He decorated it with a cotton wool trim, adding touches here and there that she wouldn't have thought of, and making it look totally effortless as he did. 'There!' he said a moment later. 'So, just,

 160

like, ninety-nine more to go!'

Angel pulled an ironic face. 'Right.'

But they got a production line going, and Angel was again surprised at how therapeutic working on something that was creative felt. She hadn't realised she was feeling a bit tense about things until she really did have a chance to relax, as Caspar had been so keen to advise her to do before ... But she never completely lost her awareness of being in the room with him, alone, with his knee almost touching hers under the desk and his fingertips brushing hers when he handed her a partially made hat, or—

'Cool, we'd better call it a day for now. I'll finish these up tomorrow,' Caspar said, pulling out his phone to check the time.

'Yeah, sure,' Angel said, trying to ignore the direction her mind had been going in. They packed up, and Caspar walked her to the front of the school. It was already dark outside, clear and cold, and as Angel pulled on her woolly hat, Caspar playfully reached over and pulled it down a bit further over one of her eyes, like he used to do to annoy her when they were kids. But this time it didn't seem quite so irritating. As she pulled it back up, Caspar's eyes lingered on hers – or was she imagining it? Wishing more like. Either way, suddenly Angel wasn't so cold.

'See you tomorrow, AG,' he said.

'Yeah.' Then she remembered something, and gave him a sly look. 'Oh, and it's your turn to make the snacks for the screening by the way! Maybe brownies or something, whatever's easiest, as well as the popcorn, or—'

'Uh . . . really?'

'Yeah, I did it last time. And you still owe me, remember?' She laughed at Caspar's pained expression. 'It's cool, you'll be fine.' She winked at him deliberately, seeing as he loved doing it to her. 'See you tomorrow!'

Caspar shook his head with a chuckle, and she could feel him watching her as she turned and walked away, smiling too.

CHAPTER 12

Wednesday 10th December

Angel crawled out of bed to hit her alarm clock, amazed that it was already hump day. Tuesday had passed in a whirl of school, gossiping with Izzy at the Crafty Cuppa after it, and then an evening spent under a pile of textbooks. The entrance exam for Dunstable Academy was exactly ten days away, and Angel was beginning to feel the pressure of it all. But there was another, much bigger reason why today felt significant. She sat up in her bed and looked at the photo in a frame next to the advent calendar on her windowsill. It was a man with strong brown arms and a big smile, holding a little toddler in his arms – her and her dad. Only a few years after that photo had been taken, he had died of a brain haemorrhage. Angel picked up the picture and smiled at it, remembering how annoying her dad had found it that his birthday was so close to Christmas. She could almost hear his deep voice saying it, though it got harder and harder with each year to remember how he had spoken, or what he had smelled like. Sighing and brushing away a tear, she put the picture down and picked up the advent calendar, scratching off its message for today.

Try to recognise people's differences as strengths.

'Going all philosophical on me today, eh?' Angel said to the calendar with a slight smile. She got ready for school and made her way downstairs to see her mum putting her coat on top of her scrubs, a stressed look her face. The boiler had been playing up again, and Angel knew that Ruth had also been asked to take a few more shifts to cover for one of her colleagues who was having some surgery next week.

'Oh, good, glad I caught you, darling. Dr Benedict just needs a copy of your passport to confirm your place in the programme at St Ted's this Saturday, and I haven't had a moment to get you to dig it out of that drawer in your room,' she said, shoving things into her bag distractedly. 'And so help me, Angel, if you've lost it—'

'I haven't, Mum! I'll take a picture on my phone and send it over to you before I go to school.' Angel was a bit put out that her mum was in stress-mode and on her way out of the door. She'd been hoping to talk to her a bit about her dad, his birthday, and some of the stuff she'd been feeling about it.

'OK, good. Oh.' Her mum came to a halt and looked over at Angel. 'There was something else I wanted to . . . err . . . run past you? Or let you know, I suppose.'

Angel looked over at her. 'Yeah?' she said warily.

'Since you're going to be away at the hospital

doing the doctor trainee day, and you'll probably be back in the evening, and I finally have a whole weekend off this week . . .'

'What is it, Mum?' From the number of caveats, Angel could already tell she wasn't going to like whatever it was.

'Well, Victor has asked if he could take me down to Brighton. His daughter's got a little art exhibition down there, and it's opening this weekend,' her mum said cautiously. 'But it would mean me being gone overnight . . . I know you're old enough now, and it's not like you're the sort to throw some wild party while I'm gone,' she added, trying for a smile, which Angel did not return.

'Right. So you're going off with Victor's family for the weekend and leaving me here?'

Angel felt bad as soon as she said it, but she was still annoyed even as her mum's face fell. 'He invited you too, darling, and he really wanted you to come, but I assumed that you'd never give up the chance of the programme at St Ted's. It really is a big favour to me that Dr Benedict is doing, so—'

Interrupting with a sigh, Angel folded her arms. 'Obviously I'm not going to give that up, but . . .' She shook her head. 'Look, whatever. It's fine. Of course it is.'

But her mum looked even more stressed at that response. 'Well, look, I'm going to be late for work, so we can talk about it later.'

'No need, Mum, honestly.' Angel struggled to sound convincing, but she was still pretty irritated about the whole thing, especially today of all days. She couldn't help it. 'I'll see you later, OK?'

As her mum rushed out of the door, Angel couldn't help feeling that things were changing too quickly for her comfort.

Angel had been marginally cheered up by Izzy's comical – and borderline too-gleeful – recounting of her stepmonster's dressing gown falling open when she answered the door to the postman that morning. But by lunchtime, Angel had told her friend she was going to grab a sandwich and head to the library. She kind of wanted a quiet space, and that was her happy place.

As she made her way through the corridor, she saw Caspar – but her heart sank when she saw who he was with. Tilda Chase sashayed smugly beside him. *Great, like today isn't bad enough!*

'Ahh, there she is!' Caspar said, grinning as they met, which sort of surprised Angel.

She noticed that Tilda had a load of strips of paper and tape in her hands, and was looking up at Caspar with a mixture of slight irritation and unbridled attraction. Angel could definitely relate.

'Tilda here offered to help out with the posters. But since it's actually our job, maybe you could give us a hand?' Caspar asked.

'I . . . I don't mind at all!' Tilda said quickly.

Angel nodded, looking between them both, suddenly wanting to capitalise on the opportunity to derail Tilda's plans for lunchtime seduction, petty as it was. 'Oh no it's cool, I can spare ten minutes or so. I was headed to the library.'

'Well, since we haven't really got time to make all-new posters because *someone* suggested another little arts and crafts exercise,' Caspar said pointedly, though his expression was light-hearted, 'we need to tape the new info on to the film posters we put up last week.' He reached down towards Tilda's hands, and Angel's eyes followed, watching as Caspar gently eased some of the supplies out of them. She stifled a sigh at the way Tilda looked at him through her eyelashes as their hands touched.

'Tilda, why don't you take the east corridor –' *Ha!* This time Angel was stifling a giggle as Tilda's face fell at Caspar's instruction – 'and . . . Oh, Sanj, mate?' Caspar called to Sanjay, who was passing them on the way to the canteen. 'Got a bit of time before you meet my so-called best mate?' he said with a grin. 'I know he won't be missing pie day at lunch, but we're on second sitting, right?'

Sanj came over, shrugging. 'Yeah, I can give you guys a hand.'

Caspar quickly explained, then suggested, 'You

can help out Tilda.' He rested a hand on her shoulder. Angel could see Tilda's mixed emotions at the attention, again feeling a bit of awkward understanding. Did Caspar even notice the effect he had? 'And Angel and I will hit the west corridor. We should be done in no time!' He went to stand beside Angel and nudged her. 'Can't keep this one away from her books for too long, you know. She'll go into withdrawal.' That wink again. What was he playing at? Maybe just using her to make Tilda jealous or something? *Yeah, right . . .*

'Go, team!' Sanj said with a laugh, and they split up in their respective directions.

'So, I've been looking up recipes,' Caspar said as they walked over to the first poster they needed to update.

'Recipes?'

'For the snacks you're forcing me to make, despite my having absolutely zero abilities in the kitchen.'

Angel scoffed. 'Oh, that's a little girly's place is it? Not somewhere a big man should be caught?'

Caspar smiled wryly and shook his head. 'Ahh,

AG, so quick to take offence,' he teased. *Ugh*. Why was he so exasperating? *And gorgeous* ... 'I was just going to get your advice on whether to make brownies, or go for blondies instead?'

Caspar held out a hand and she passed him some tape. He stuck the new piece of paper over the poster and they moved on to the next one as they talked.

'They're not that great, in my opinion,' Angel said.

Caspar paused and looked at her in a way that made her feel a bit self-conscious. 'Yeah, blondies aren't really my thing, either.'

Angel blushed from the tips of her toes to the top of her head, and only noticed Caspar was waiting for the next bit of tape after an embarrassingly long silence. She was still desperately searching for a way to move on from his flirtatious comment – *if it even* was *flirtatious?* – when they heard a noise coming from further down the hallway.

'She just collapsed!'

'What's happening?'

'Should we—'

Angel and Caspar rushed over, to see a girl on the ground with a few of their fellow students gathering around her. 'Clear back, give her some room,' Caspar said, and everyone seemed to listen to the authority in his voice.

Angel knelt down close, and managed to catch sight of what she was looking for as the girl fitted – a bracelet on her arm. 'Medical Alert – Epilepsy' it read. Angel dredged her mind, trying to picture her textbooks which said what to do when someone had an epileptic fit.

'We should move her,' someone said anxiously, but Angel shook her head, reaching for the girl cautiously.

'No,' Angel said, loosening the girl's tie. 'She's safe here, it'll be OK. I just want to make sure this isn't too restrictive.'

Caspar moved in front of them. 'Guys, let's give her a bit of space, yeah? Maybe go and grab a teacher and get them to call an ambulance? Angel's got this.' He glanced down at her admiringly. 'We'll stay with her.'

The girl's convulsions began to slow, and then eventually stopped as Caspar crouched down beside her. 'Help me turn her onto her side,' Angel said. Even with such a shocking situation, she couldn't help her heart racing even more than it already was as she realised how close Caspar was, leaning over the girl to roll her. Their foreheads were almost touching. 'Carefully,' Angel added, but Caspar was already handling the girl with movements that seemed almost practised.

The girl's eyes slowly began to open, and she looked very upset. Angel wasn't sure what to say, but immediately Caspar was rubbing the girl's arm gently and talking in soothing tones, asking her name. He looked up for a moment as one of his football mates, Malcolm Connelly, walked past the scene, smirking – the deadly look Caspar shot him shut the boy up swiftly. Then Caspar turned back to their 'patient', smoothing back her hair and taking off his jumper to cushion her head.

'Heather? Good to meet you. Now listen there's no need to be so dramatic, you know? Nobody likes an attention seeker,' he joked gently, still smoothing her hair. The girl managed a smile. 'Don't worry, all right? You're going to be OK. Someone's on the way.' Angel saw Caspar's shoulders sag in relief as the school nurse hurried down the corridor towards them, with a paramedic in tow.

'Thank you,' Heather managed quietly, and Caspar stood up, then offered Angel a hand to help her up, too. He held on to her hand a moment after she had stood, and she could feel that there was a slight tremble in his grip. She squeezed his hand tighter, and he looked at her, exhaling lightly as he let go. Angel wasn't sure where to look. They quickly explained what had happened, and then more paramedics arrived with a stretcher, though Angel was relieved to see that Heather was able to get onto it herself without too much trouble.

'Wow. That was . . .'

'Intense,' Caspar finished, nodding.

'You were really good with her,' Angel observed sincerely. 'Like you . . . Kind of knew what it might be like to face stuff like that?' Her mind suddenly drifted to his sister.

Caspar wouldn't meet her eye. 'Just doing what anyone would have done,' he said. 'I . . . I don't have experience of that specifically . . .' He shrugged and took a deep breath. 'Anyway, better finish these off, eh?' He gestured to the next poster as they made their way in the direction they had been walking.

He seemed a bit preoccupied now, but Angel couldn't blame him. They reached the final poster, which happened to be outside the library, and Angel nodded to the door. 'Guess I'll get in there, then,' she said.

To her surprise, Caspar asked, 'Mind if I join you for a bit? I could do with somewhere quiet after . . .' He gestured back down the hallway. 'All that.'

'Yeah, OK,' she said, feeling oddly shy as Caspar held the door open for her.

Angel inhaled the smell of the books as they entered the library, and led them to a quiet corner table by the window. Angel got her textbooks out and opened her sandwich. She could see Caspar eyeing it, so handed him half, and he finally grinned. It was good to see his smile back.

'You should probably, I dunno, do a bit of studying?' she said, pointing at her own books with a smile of her own. Caspar pushed his chair back and made a show of scanning the shelves near their table. But a moment later he actually looked interested in something.

'Ahh. The Don!' he said, pulling a big book off a shelf. Angel read the name on the cover: *Marc Chagall*. 'His art is . . . *incredible*.' Caspar said, putting the book down on their table and opening it up reverently. He looked through the index, then turned to a page eagerly. 'This one's my favourite. Check it out,' he said, his eyes wide. Angel tried to angle her head, but couldn't see it properly, so got up and went around to the same side of the desk as Caspar, leaning down and trying not to inhale the warm scent of his . . . was it body spray, or aftershave? Or just . . . him?

Caspar tapped the page, and they both studied the image. 'It's called *Job*. It's actually a tapestry. This doctor asked Chagall to make it, she was head of a big rehabilitation institution in the States,' Caspar said softly. 'She thought his art was all about hope and faith. And it was. I mean, he decided to make this tapestry as a symbol of optimism for the people using the rehabilitation centre. Job is the patron saint of people with disabilities.' Angel glanced at Caspar, who was staring intently at the picture. She looked back at it, absorbing the meaning. It seemed to mean a lot to Caspar as well. 'Chagall saw blue as the colour of hope, too,' he added. 'Which is why it's my favourite colour.' He gave a gentle smile as he turned to Angel, looking into her eyes intently.

'It's beautiful,' she whispered, though she wasn't looking at the image of the tapestry. Suddenly, she thought of the message in her advent calendar this morning, and what had happened with Heather and now this. Through Caspar's eyes she was beginning to see the strengths in people's so-called differences. It all felt so symbolic – and so related to the reason they were raising money for the hospice, even to why she was so determined to become a doctor. A tiny part of Angel wondered if her dad was looking down on her today, showing her some signs. She liked to think so. And she liked staring into Caspar's eyes ... Even if thinking of her dad today had reminded her of how Casper had stopped being her friend at the exact time she needed him most. She hadn't just lost one person important to her – she'd lost two.

They both jumped and looked away as the bell rang to indicate it was almost the end of lunch.

'Uh ...' Caspar closed the book, swallowing hard. 'Sorry most of your lunch got taken up. Thanks for letting me come to your little library sanctuary,' he said, turning away to put the book on the shelf. Angel had got no studying done – again – but this felt more important.

'No worries,' she said softly.

CHAPTER 13

Thursday 11th December

'Cut, cut, cut,' Izzy shouted over the cacophony around them. Angel sighed and she and Ola ran back over to her. They peered over Izzy's shoulder to look at the footage she'd shot on her phone.

'Yeah, we need to see more of my face,' Ola said, nodding intently. Along with the skating rink, the winter fair had rides. A Ferris wheel, a roller coaster, games stalls and twinkling Christmas lights had been set up in the park, and the place was swarming with people and noise. Ola had decided that to add to her acting show reel, she would – in record time! – put together a short film using the fair as her backdrop. Angel wasn't quite sure how she'd got roped into participating in front of the camera, but Izzy was taking her directorial duties pretty seriously.

'Back to one! Places, guys!'

But after another go, and a growing, irritated line at the pellet gun range, they decided that 'action heroine' wasn't quite the angle that Ola should take for her film debut.

'Maybe something more romantic?' Ola said. 'But we need a leading man . . .'

Just as she spoke, Izzy let out a squeal. 'OK, don't look. OK, look. But, like, don't. Subtly, OK?'

Angel and Ola ignored her, and stared in the direction she had indicated. They saw Manny and Sanj striding towards them, laughing with an older man and woman that Angel assumed were their parents. They paused by a caramel apple stand, and Sanj and Manny pointed towards the Ferris wheel, while their parents shook their heads.

'Great, why don't we see if Sanj might be up for a bit of acting? He's definitely got movie star looks,' Angel said, already holding up a hand to wave at him. Izzy's eyes grew wider with each step Sanj and Manny made towards them, until Angel feared they might actually pop out of her head.

'Hey, guys,' Sanj said as they came to a halt in front of Angel, Izzy and Ola. 'You remember my brother, Manny?'

Angel stifled a laugh as Izzy made a frankly indescribable noise in greeting. She nudged Ola, who quickly, and in typically dramatic fashion, explained her acting goals, and her vision for the short film. 'Cool, doing a bit of directing, then?' Manny said to Izzy, who then appeared to stop breathing. Angel edged a foot over to gently step on Izzy's toe to prompt her, and her friend finally cleared her throat to speak.

'Yeah. I mean, who knows, I could be the next Ava Duvernay if this goes well, right?' Izzy managed, and Angel actually felt proud of her! 'Err, I was thinking, Sanj, you could play Ola's leading man, taking a ride on the Ferris wheel? And Ange, if you shoot some footage from on the ground, I could get on the wheel and get some close ups from there? I know you hate heights.'

'Facts!' Angel said. 'Sounds like a plan.'

'Well, we were heading to the Ferris wheel anyway,' Manny said, smiling at Izzy. 'I'll help out with the filming up there. We could get in the pod behind these two and . . .'

Angel could tell that Izzy's brain had gone into meltdown at the very fact that Manny was speaking to her, let alone that he was suggesting they get into a Ferris wheel pod – a *two-person* pod – together.

'Excellent!' Angel said, getting her phone out. They all walked towards the ride and handed the guy operating it their tokens. She gave Izzy a thumbs-up when Manny was looking in a different direction, and then they all clambered in to the pods. Izzy mimed an *eek* at Angel, but then quickly called 'action'.

As Angel filmed some shots of their ride from the ground, though, she noticed a message pop up on her screen.

HELLLLP!! Is baking powder the same thing as baking soda? I have no idea what I'm doing. Strong possibility of poisoning our fellow students. HEELLLLP!!

Angel laughed. It was from Caspar! She had never really messaged with him before but, forgetting she was meant to be filming, she replied. After all, the challenge on her advent calendar this morning had said:

Put others before yourself today.

Not that she would have required much persuading to offer Caspar some help.

I *suppose* I can come over and give you a hand. I'm just at the winter fair, could be there pretty quick.

The moment she sent it, she wondered if that was too forward. Would she actually go round to

Caspar's house? But she was dying to spend more time with him, she couldn't deny it. She sighed in relief as she got a message back.

YES YES YES! You're a life-saver. But then, they don't call you Angel for nothing, I guess!

She blushed at her screen and typed a reply, just as the Ferris wheel swung to a halt.

See you in ten or so.

Ola and Sanj were high-fiving each other, clearly pleased with their acting abilities, and Izzy looked stunned as Manny helped her out of her pod. 'How did it look from down here?' Ola asked eagerly.

'Err, great!' Angel said. She thought she had filmed a couple of moments that might be usable anyway. 'Listen, guys, I said I'd pop round to Caspar's for a bit and help him out with some of the snacks for the film screening tomorrow.'

'Oh yeah?' Izzy said, coming out of her Manny fog long enough to raise an eyebrow at her friend.

'Yeah,' Angel replied. 'But you guys have fun here, *all of you*,' she said pointedly, and Izzy nodded, relenting. She clearly understood the irony of having an excuse to spend time with a crush, even if they hadn't really talked about what was going on with Angel and her probably-painfully-one-sided crush on Caspar yet.

But she found herself getting increasingly nervous with each step of the once-familiar five-minute walk from the fair to Caspar's house. As she stood on the doorstep, she took several deep breaths before she pressed the doorbell, then chuckled in spite of her nerves, remembering the music that it played instead of the traditional chimes. It took her back to her childhood in a way that sort of made her relax a bit. Until Caspar flung the door open, and she noticed the chaos behind him.

'Oh, thank God you're here,' he said by way of greeting.

He had flour in his hair and dusted on one cheek, and his hands appeared to be smeared with chocolate, as did the white T-shirt he was wearing, and the dishtowel that he had tucked into the waistband of his black jeans. He looked delicious, disheveled and desperate. Angel had to clear her throat to speak.

'No worries,' she said, as Caspar stepped aside to let her in.

'Here, let me take your coat,' he said, and she began unbuttoning it, surprised as he wiped his hands on the dishcloth then moved behind her to help it off her shoulders. As he hung it up, she moved away shyly. Angel hadn't been to Caspar's house in years, and it was both comfortingly familiar and strangely surreal to be there.

She couldn't help thinking fondly about her dad, shouting at the TV with Caspar's as they watched the West Indies play cricket on TV. Some of the furniture was a bit different, but as always there were lots of paintings on the wall, a sewing machine set up in one corner, and shoes and coats and clothes everywhere. The Johnsons had never been super-tidy, which Angel supposed explained some of Caspar's relaxed approach to life. She'd loved the cosy chaos of their house when she was a kid, and it still filled her with warmth and memories now. She was curious, though, about a set of crutches that were propped up by the door. But she had little time to think about them as Caspar strode away through the living room and into the kitchen, glancing eagerly behind him to make sure Angel was keeping up.

The kitchen looked like a firework had gone off in it. There were packages of flour, sugar, open bars of chocolate everywhere, as well as recipe books open to various pages, and what seemed like the entire contents of the crockery cupboards and cutlery drawers piled in the sink. A burning smell was coming from the oven.

'I. Cannot. Bake,' Caspar intoned, standing in the middle of the disaster zone and throwing his hands into the air.

Angel laughed, and walked over to him,

reaching up without thinking to place her hands on his shoulders. It was only as they connected that she felt the strong muscles under her hands – and felt the wave of self-consciousness wash over her. But they were there now, and she needed to get a handle on this situation.

'Relax, Johnson,' she said, even as she could feel his shoulders tensing more. She wasn't sure now if it was the exasperation over his failed baking efforts, or something else, but she stared up into his eyes and continued her supposed pep-talk. 'I said relax,' she repeated, moving her hands away from his shoulders more slowly than she had intended.

'I'm trying to,' he said, his voice deep, and a half-smile on his lips. His lips . . . Angel looked down, realising her feet were awfully close to his. She took a step back, avoiding his eyes and glancing around the kitchen again.

'First things first – we need to take whatever is charring away in that oven out, and clean this place up.' She turned the oven off, opened it, and fanned away the smoke that billowed out at her. The moment she did it, Angel knew it was a mistake.

'Oh careful, it might set the—'

A shrill, piercing sound began assailing their ears. 'Smoke alarm off?' she shouted, finishing Caspar's sentence, and they both laughed. She ran to open the back door, letting a gust of wintery air in, and Caspar grabbed an empty baking tray and began fanning the alarm that was on the ceiling in the middle of the living room. Angel tried and failed not to observe his abs as his T-shirt lifted while he reached up towards it. Finally, the screeching stopped.

'So this has been a relaxing Thursday night so far,' Caspar said with another laugh, flopping onto the sofa beneath the alarm. Angel came over and sat beside him for a moment.

'We can do this,' she said. 'It's going to be no sweat, you'll see.'

'There's already been a fair bit of sweat, AG, let me tell you.' He turned to her. 'How was the fair?

Thanks for dragging yourself away from it for me,' he said, still eyeing her.

Angel shrugged. 'I was being roped into some filmmaking exercise with my mates that was getting a bit out of hand, so it's cool.'

'I won't ask,' Caspar said, sitting up so that their knees were almost touching.

To distract herself, Angel reached out to dip her hands into the bowl of decorative glass beads that had always sat on the Johnson's coffee table. 'I remember these,' she said with a nostalgic smile. 'I also remember you getting one stuck up your nose that time . . .'

'Dunno what you're talking about,' Caspar said with a grin, standing up then offering her a hand. She took it gingerly and he pulled her up, then hung on to her hand, like he had before. 'It's nice having you back here, Angel,' he said, then let go and moved off to the kitchen, as if he was trying to diffuse the moment. Angel thought about mentioning the fact that he had been the one to outgrow their friendship, but as she watched him staring around the kitchen again helplessly, she decided to take charge.

'OK. You wash everything up,' she said, walking over to close the back door with a shiver. 'I'll get rid of this burnt up nuclear waste and clean off the surfaces. Then we'll start from scratch.'

In about half an hour, they had managed to get the kitchen back to a useable state.

'So where are your mum and dad while this apocalypse has been happening?' Angel asked as she gathered the ingredients for brownies together again, this time in an organised manner.

'Oh they're both at the hos—' He stopped himself. 'Err, they're out of the house with my sister Ruby this evening.'

Angel paused in measuring out the flour to stroll over to the fridge, where she could see a few drawings attached with magnets. A couple of them she recognised as being Caspar's; the sketches were intricate and startlingly realistic. And then there were others that looked like they were by a much younger hand. 'Did she do these?' Angel asked, pointing and smiling at his pictures.

'What, you don't think they're up to my usual standard?' Caspar joked, but she could see his pride as he looked at his sister's actual handiwork.

'It's weird to think that you've had a whole little sister in the time since I used to hang out here,' Angel said.

Caspar walked over and lifted up a magnet to look more closely at one of his sister's drawings, with a pensive look on his face. 'Yeah. Apparently she was a bit of a surprise.' He smiled. 'An amazing one.'

'How old is she now?' Angel asked.

Caspar sighed lightly as he returned the drawing to its place on the fridge door. 'Just turned six,' he said. Angel didn't want to press, even though she was dying to ask more, especially about whether Ruby was still having the health issues she remembered hearing about when they were just moving up to high school. Of course, by then she and Caspar hadn't really been mates any more . . .

Instead, she returned to measuring out the ingredients, and showing Caspar how to blend them and melt the chocolate. She tried to ignore the mischievous look on his face as he stirred, but she knew he was plotting something. He lifted the wooden spoon he was stirring it with out of the bowl, and swept some chocolate onto his finger.

'What are you up to?' Angel said, eyeing him warily.

'Oh just . . .' He paused, then dapped the finger on to her nose. 'That.'

Angel stood with her hands on her hips, the warm aroma of chocolate assailing her nostrils. 'Mature.'

'I thought so.'

She chuckled in spite of herself, and went to grab a paper towel to wipe it off, but Caspar objected. 'Don't waste precious chocolate,' he said. He swiped the chocolate off her nose, and offered his finger to her, holding it in front of her mouth. Angel's gaze moved from his finger to his eyes, and back again. Closing her eyes, she moved forward, and jolted as she felt his finger nudge her lips. She licked them, and opened her eyes again just in time to see Caspar suck the remnants off of his fingertip.

Chocolate had literally never tasted so good in Angel's entire *life*!

'Let's, um . . . We should get these in the oven,' she said hoarsely, feeling hot. Turning away and unwinding the Secret Santa hairband from her wrist, she used it to push her braids off her face quickly.

'I like that,' Caspar said, nodding towards her head.

Angel smiled. 'Yeah, believe it or not, it was from my Secret Santa,' she said.

'Is that right? Good taste.' Caspar poured the brownie mixture into the three trays they'd lined up. They had twenty-five minutes to wait while the treats baked, so Caspar turned on the TV, and they laughed and joked, critiquing the programme until the timer went off. By the time they'd taken the brownies out to cool, it was getting late.

'Whoa, I'd better be getting home actually,'

Angel said, checking her phone. She ignored the teasing messages from Izzy and Ola, and sent a quick one to her mum explaining where she was and that she was heading home, in case Ruth had rung their landline during her night shift – Angel knew she was the only one likely to have tried it. She kept trying to convince her mum to get rid of it.

'I'll walk you,' Caspar said.

'No, no it's fine,' Angel began to protest, but Caspar shook his head. He pulled on the trainers he'd left strewn by the door and his coat, then helped Angel into hers, like he'd helped her with it earlier. She felt almost shy as they stepped out in the cold air, walking close together as though for warmth, but really because of something Angel couldn't quite explain. She watched their breath form in clouds in front of them as they walked along the path to the high street and towards Angel's house. It was like their friendship was starting again, but also . . . No, nothing more than that probably. She'd take it though, whatever it was. But she knew she had to keep her expectations low – no use risking getting hurt all over again.

'Between the elf hats and those brownies, we'd better sell out the screening tomorrow,' Caspar said, and Angel turned to him.

'I reckon we will, you know. We make a pretty good team, Johnson.'

'We do,' Caspar said, his face a little in shadow under the street lights. They walked on in charged silence, until they reached the bottom of the little walkway up to Angel's house. She opened the gate, and rested her hand on it.

'No, no, no, this is a door-to-door service,' Caspar said, gesturing for her to walk up the path, and following on behind. Angel jumped a little as the security light clicked on when they reached her doorstep. 'Thanks so much for coming and saving my behind tonight, Angel. I don't know how I'll repay you.'

Angel held her chin, feigning that she was thinking something up. 'There will definitely be some menial tasks I can think of forcing you to do,' she said with a chuckle. She'd taken off her hairband, but forgotten to put on her hat, so her braids were falling into her face again. Suddenly, she saw that Caspar had taken off his glove, and his warm hand moved towards her, sweeping a couple of plaits back and brushing against her cheek in the process. For one split second, she thought he might be leaning in to kiss her . . .

'Well, I really appreciate what you did,' Caspar said, his voice low. 'And I won't let you down tomorrow.' Before she knew what was happening, Caspar opened his arms, and she unthinkingly stepped forward into his hug. She took a deep breath of his warm, comforting scent, and he squeezed her a little tighter. 'See you tomorrow, Angel,' he whispered, his voice muffled as he leaned into her. She exhaled with a mixture of sorrow and relief and pure giddiness as he finally let go. He pivoted on his heel, and she watched him head down the path, turning slightly to give her a little salute as he closed the gate.

She let herself inside her house and leaned back against the door as she closed it.

'That ...' she murmured dreamily to herself, still smelling the lingering scent of Caspar on her coat, 'was *so much better* than a kiss.'

CHAPTER 14

Friday 12th December

Angel had fully expected a moodier response to her last-minute ticket sales push from her classmates as they entered the school, but she was really happy to be wrong. To be fair, the sound of the choir was lifting her mood, too! Even though she had to admit it was still pretty high after last night and her embrace with Caspar . . .

Angel joined in cheerily with the final few lines as they rounded off a rousing acapella rendition of 'Santa Claus is Coming to Town', and then lifted her dwindling roll of tickets again. 'Last few tickets for the film screening tonight,' she called as people trickled in through the front doors. 'Come and see *Elf* and help us raise money for the Bluebell Hospice! You won't regret it!' She smiled as Izzy and Ola sidled up to her.

'Yes, Ange, giving me market trader chic!' Izzy said, even though Angel was wearing her normal coat and hat – though having seen Caspar's, she had dug out her mum's old fingerless gloves to make it easier to tear off tickets and take money. Out of the corner of her eye, she saw Sanj – who seemed to be leading the singers – confer with his fellow choristers, and then they launched into a gospel number that got Angel's toes tapping again. Izzy and Ola stepped aside as she sold three more tickets to some Year Eights. At the rate they were going, the screening would definitely sell out!

After everything that had happened, she was almost certain that Caspar wasn't going to flake out on them again, but there was a tiny worry still in the back of her mind about it. So she was relieved – in more ways than one – to see him stroll up a couple of minutes later, box of brownies in hand, with Josh.

'Laptop's in here, all ready to go for later,' he told Angel with a grin, while Josh seemed distracted, applauding the choir enthusiastically as they finished off another number. He gave a dude-like finger point towards Sanj, followed by a thumbs-up. It was really great to see everyone getting behind the last-minute push for some final ticket sales, but Angel was mainly distracted by her even-more-acute awareness of Caspar. 'It took everything I had not to eat all of these last night,' he was saying, moving closer to her behind the ticket stall they'd set up, and popping the Tupperware down to lift the lid proudly. 'You smashed it!'

'*We* did! These should sell like hot cakes!'

'Or . . . room temperature brownies,' he said.

'I set you up for that.'

'OK, well—' Their bantering was interrupted by the bell for school to start. Angel still felt a weird buzz at how friendly things were getting with Caspar as they went their separate ways for their first lessons – and Izzy was *not* looking to avoid the subject.

'I definitely called this,' she said, nodding sagely. 'He's into you.'

'He's not . . . into me. He's just being nice. He, like, wants to be friends again or something I think,' Angel said as they sat down to a painful stretch of double geography. 'Anyway, I think he's seeing Tilda Chase.'

Izzy pulled a face. 'Ugh. Well, if he's not *into you* into you, he's an idiot,' her friend affirmed. 'I think you two are really cute together.'

'This isn't the best time for me have anything like that going on anyway, Izz,' Angel said awkwardly. She wasn't entirely sure if she believed what she was saying or was just embarrassed at the fact she actually fancied someone. Especially *who* it was she fancied. 'I need to focus on the Dunstable Academy exam which is only just over a week away, plus the fact that I'm off on this course this weekend at the hospital. *And* I have to contend with my mother being practically halfway down the aisle with this guy we hardly know . . .'

Izzy nodded sceptically, and seemed about to respond when Mr Yardley walked in and called the room to order in his typically dull manner. *To be continued*, Izzy scrawled on her notebook and showed it to Angel. She had no doubt it would be!

The rest of the day flew by, even with Izzy analysing all of Caspar's behaviour towards Angel over lunchtime. Angel was actually pretty excited about the film screening that evening. She was also smug about having found another Secret Santa present for Josh – one that didn't cost too much money. She had a spare USB stick, and in the last fifteen minutes of lunch she had headed to a library computer to copy a playlist of gospel songs on to it, seeing as he'd been so into the choir that morning. Perfect! She'd slipped it into his locker while he was play-fighting with a couple of the other boys with his locker open after school.

Now, they were putting the final touches to the set up for the screening, and as she unfolded the last of the chairs in the assembly hall, she smiled (trying to avoid it being a goofy one) watching Caspar working with a couple of the computer science guys to set up the projector. Everything was going according to plan for once. Soon the doors were open, and everyone began taking their seats for the screening. Angel and Olivia were tasked with handing out the elf hats that she and Caspar had made, although she was a little disappointed not to be working with him on selling the snacks. A gaggle of girls had crowded the table, and she could tell the brownies would be gone in a matter of minutes as he flattered and flirted with them. She shook her head a little to herself. As *if* she'd ever stand any kind of romantic chance with Caspar Johnson. She was still getting used to the idea that she'd *want* to.

Still, everyone began to take their seats, and

Angel finally felt like she had an excuse to go over to Caspar as he did a final check on his laptop.

'All ready to go?' she asked.

'Yup,' he said, signalling to Josh to dim the lights. He hit play and everyone applauded as the film started. Quietly, Caspar pulled over a chair and gestured for Angel to sit down, then got another for himself and sat down next to her. She could feel the warmth of his body next to her in the dark, and it took everything she had to concentrate on the film. But as they got to the scene when everyone starts singing in Central Park, she realised that Sanj had come up with another great idea. The members of the choir, all dotted around the hall, stood up and began to sing along with the song on screen! It created a really magical effect, and everyone clapped again at the end of it. But when Angel turned to Caspar to see his reaction, she noticed that instead of concentrating on the choir and the film, his face was illuminated by his phone screen. He was frowning hard.

'Everything OK?' she whispered, and Caspar glanced over at her.

'Yeah, fine,' he replied dismissively, looking back at his phone with an expression that suggested that was definitely not true. He typed out a quick response to whatever he'd read, then shoved his phone back into his pocket with an anxious, faraway look in his eyes. Angel was perplexed, and starting to get a bit annoyed again. Something was definitely up, but clearly Caspar wasn't interested in talking about it. What kind of so-called friendship was that? Why he just kept saying things were fine when they obviously weren't she didn't know, but she was tired of him being all friendly one second, then dismissive the next. Was this just the way he was – good for fun and nothing more serious? She sat next to him in an awkward, irritated, anxious silence, wondering if he'd rather be somewhere else. Anywhere but there with her, at least. His folded arms and hunched body language certainly suggested as much.

As soon as the film was over, Caspar began

packing up his stuff without saying anything. Angel tried not to sulk as some of the council members gathered at the back of the hall. Everyone else started filtering out, laughing and joking with festive cheer after the film. Angel was feeling a bit deflated, to say the least.

'Excellent job, Caspar,' Tilda said, heading straight over to him and rubbing his arm. 'Oh, and Angel, Sanj, you really pulled that out of the bag. Nice one. The next event is going to be even bigger. Maybe we can try to fit a few more seats in, sell more tickets? Mrs Black has already let me know how impressed she is with the council this term, so you guys should all be really proud.' Angel noticed that Tilda was still looking at Caspar as she spoke, but at least he didn't seem to be paying her much attention either.

'You're right, we'd have been nowhere without Caspar on this one,' Angel said, trying to see if she'd get any reaction. She looked over at him, but he just threw her a quick, unconvincing smile while shoving his laptop into his bag.

'I've got to go,' he mumbled, then glanced at Josh, whose concerned look made Angel even more puzzled. What could be going on? She wasn't sure what came over her, but she was determined not to let Caspar leaving in a hurry be some strange enigma *again*. She said a quick goodbye to everyone, and gave Izzy and Ola a hug, only vaguely hearing their congratulations in her eagerness to follow Caspar.

Angel rounded a corner out in the corridor and caught up with him in the slightly darkened hallway as he stopped to put something back in his locker.

'Hey!' she called out, cringing a bit as her voice echoed around the empty space. Caspar turned, seeming startled. Angel pressed on. 'What's going on? Aren't you glad things went so well?'

Caspar zipped up his bag and shut his locker. ''Course I am. Listen, Angel, I have to go.'

'You always do! Why are you being so mysterious all the time, eh?' They stood inches apart now, Angel aware of her breathing as she'd rushed to catch up to him.

'I'm not,' Caspar mumbled, avoiding her eyes even in the gloom of the corridor.

'I thought . . .' Angel began, then stopped.

Caspar did look at her then. 'You thought what?' he said in a low voice. Suddenly he didn't seem in such a hurry to leave, and Angel's heart quickened even more.

'That we were starting to be friends again,' she finished weakly.

'We are.'

Angel folded her arms and shook her head. 'Not with the way you're acting. And I'm not that same kid who will just let you tread all over our friendship any more, Caspar.'

He took a step back, frowning. 'What are you talking about?'

'When we got here.' She gestured vaguely around them. 'To high school. Suddenly you didn't want to know, and all I was good for was doing your homework or whatever. Even though . . . even though I really needed a friend then.' She had a frown herself now, remembering the hurt all over again. 'You got cool, you got popular or whatever, and I got left behind as the geeky loser girl you used to know.'

'That's . . .' Caspar seemed genuinely taken aback. His arms moved emphatically in the air as he said, 'That couldn't be further from the truth, Angel. I mean, what are you talking about? *You're* the one who changed. First of all, when we were still in primary, you pushed me away when . . . when your dad died.' His eyes were warm, almost pleading as he looked at her. 'I tried to talk about it, but you always changed the subject. Then you got on that fast-track to academic superstardom and made it clear you had no time for the likes of me. So yeah, I adapted, I stuck to my sports and being the so-called cheeky guy everyone likes. I keep some things to myself, even from you. It's my business, OK? If I hide my love for art, or wanting to go to art school, or I hide . . . Look, it's not the time for this, AG.' He exhaled, like he was genuinely upset.

'Don't call me that,' she mumbled, feeling bad even as she said it.

'I have to go,' he ground out with a finality that made Angel's heart sink. Why had she decided to confront him on all of that now, when things had been going so well? She watched him leave, staring at his rapidly receding back as he jogged outside into the cold wintery night.

When Angel finally got outside herself and turned the corner, she saw Caspar still a way up ahead of her, walking quickly with his long-legged strides. Reluctant to call out after him again even though she hated the way they'd just left things, she carried on quietly behind him. But when she reached the corner where she expected that he would have turned towards his house, she saw him jogging on ahead again, towards the sounds of the Winter Fayre. Angel was disappointed at quite how jealous she felt. Was he meeting someone – was this all some ruse so he could sneak off and meet Tilda there later?

Angel Green, when will you learn? she asked herself. Getting back a friendship with Caspar, let alone anything more, had seemed so unlikely to begin with after everything that had happened. Losing her dad, she and Caspar growing apart . . . Angel felt her heart sink and her embarrassment and confusion grow at their confrontation in the hallway, but although her pace slowed, she couldn't help keeping an eye on his figure getting smaller as he skirted around the crowd and towards where they had been selling Christmas trees the other day. She had to admit, curiosity was getting the better of her. Where was he going, if not to the fair?

As Angel followed on, it dawned on her – he was heading to the Bluebell Hospice.

'What the . . .?' she whispered to herself, shoving her hands into her pockets and moving faster to try and see if what she had concluded was true. But yes – as she got closer, she saw Caspar's tall frame heading down the walkway and in through the building's sliding doors. Just as he did, Angel saw her mother heading towards the doors, too. She had her coat on over her scrubs, and her handbag on her shoulder. Glancing at the time, Angel realised her mum must be on the way out at the end of today's shift. When she came across Caspar, they both stopped, and Angel watched as he seemed to be asking Ruth something anxiously. Her mum put her hands on his arms, then slid them down to grasp his hands. She could tell by her mother's expression that she was reassuring him, and then to Angel's surprise, once again her mum reached up to pull Caspar into a tight hug. Why on earth were they so close? What was he doing there, and why had neither of them told Angel anything about being in touch with one another after the families had seemed to grow apart when her dad died?

Angel felt all sorts of emotions warring within her. Something serious was obviously happening, something that would bring Caspar to the hospice. In the back of her mind, she had a feeling it was to do with his sister, but Angel was angry that there was some secret between them and she knew nothing about it. She watched as her mother released Caspar, with a final one of her trademark smiles and probably a little joke, which made Caspar smile a bit too. He headed away down the hallway, and Angel tried to move off quickly as her mum came out through the sliding doors, but—

'Angel! What are you doing here, darling?' her mum called, spotting her at the top of the path leading to the hospice.

'Err . . . We just finished with the film screening, so I thought I'd walk round this way and see if you were done, too. Good timing!'

Her mum walked over and studied her daughter's face for a moment. 'OK, that's nice, love. Yes, very good timing. I've been thinking of you a lot today – it being dad's birthday and all.'

'I thought you might have forgotten what day it was.'

'Of course I didn't forget. How could I?' Mum linked her arm through Angel's. 'Just because I'm seeing Victor, it doesn't mean I don't still miss James.'

Angel's eyes filled with tears. She knew it was a big deal for her mum even to say Dad's name. She hardly ever remembered her saying it out loud in the years since he'd died. 'I miss him too, Mum.'

'He'd be so proud of you, darling. By the way, how did it go this evening?'

Angel told her mum all about most of it, leaving out her confrontation with Caspar, but inside she was dying to ask about what she'd just seen. Rationally, she knew her mother couldn't tell her anything confidential about patients, no matter who they were, plus she didn't want to give away the fact that she'd followed Caspar.

But somehow, Angel planned to find out exactly what was going on.

CHAPTER 15

Saturday 13th December

Angel was already sitting bolt upright when her alarm went off at six o'clock in the morning the next day. She had a big plan to put everything else behind her, and do some cramming that would kill two birds with one stone by recapping a load of her physics and biology revision for her Dunstable Academy exam next Saturday, *and* simultaneously do some prep for the course at St Ted's, which she couldn't quite believe was today. This was the day she'd actually get to have some hands-on experience of being a doctor!

If she was honest, Angel had expected to be feeling unadulterated joy at the prospect. Inevitably, she'd struggled to fall asleep last night thinking about all the weirdness with Caspar at the hospice with her mum. Not to mention that today was the day her mum would be off to Brighton with Victor for his daughter's art launch or whatever it was ... *And*, Angel thought with a sigh as she checked her phone messages from last night, all this studying and the fundraising business had meant she'd had less time to just hang out with her friends. She smiled at the message from Izzy wishing her luck today, jealous at a selfie Angel noticed that she and Ola had posted online from an apparently spontaneous sleepover last night. *Missing our third musketeer ...* read the caption, along with Angel's handle and many, many hashtags, as was Izzy's style.

'It's fine,' Angel said quietly to herself, in pep-talk mode. 'Just get through this weekend, and next weekend ...'

Then it would be the Christmas holidays and everything would settle down. Well, she had no idea where she would be with the whole Caspar situation by then, but at least she'd have got the entrance exam out of the way. Although, then would commence the worry about whether she'd actually get in. She shook her head, shaking off the thought. For now, she'd just concentrate on the first hurdle. Reaching down to grab her books, she fell into the familiar, oddly comforting pattern of her studying, almost jumping when she heard a soft knock on her bedroom door.

'Brought you a cuppa,' her mum said, easing the door open and resting her new favourite mug on her bedside table. Mariah beamed over at her, making Angel smile back a little. Maybe things weren't *all* bad. 'Big day today, then,' Ruth said, moving back to lean against Angel's bedroom doorframe, hands pushed into the pockets of her dressing gown.

Angel glanced at her mum and nodded, lifting her mug to take a sip. She realised her mum must have got straight up to make her tea – her afro wasn't combed out yet, she was yawning, and dark circles under her eyes were making her look worn and tired. Angel hated that a tiny part of her hoped she would decide not to go to Brighton after all, and instead be here when Angel got home to hear all about how things had gone at St Ted's. She knew her mum deserved a break. It was rubbish feeling so at war when it came to her emotions about her mum and Victor and the whole thing. Especially so soon after her dad's birthday.

'Gosh, I'd better get in the shower,' her mum said, adding tentatively, 'Victor's picking me up at eight thirty so we can get down to Brighton in good time to meet his daughter for brunch.'

Angel nodded, then pretended to be deeply engrossed in highlighting something in her textbook. She only looked up as she felt her mattress depress. Her mum sat down next to her, bending her head to catch Angel's eye.

'I know I've said this before, sweetheart, but I'm so proud of you. I know you're going to absolutely crush this opportunity at the hospital today.'

'*Crush* it?' Angel said, feigning a cringe even as she chuckled at her mum's choice of phrase.

'Yes,' Ruth said with a smile. 'And I know it's an adjustment, but we'll figure out a new rhythm with me seeing Victor and stuff. It's probably awkward for you and . . .' She tailed off.

Angel knew things had been really hard for Ruth too, and she deserved some happiness. She reached over and squeezed her mum's hand. 'You go and have a brilliant time, Mum. Suck up some sea air, look at this chick's art or whatever . . .' She wasn't going to lay it on *too* thick! But she meant it when she said, 'And have some time to relax. I'll be totally fine here. Thank you so much for hooking things up with Dr Benedict. This opportunity will be well and truly crushed! And then the house party guests show up here tonight at seven thirty, so . . .'

'Har har,' her mum retorted, but reached over and squeezed Angel into a fiercely tight hug.

Eventually, she stood up. 'At this rate, you'll be teaching the doctors a thing or two!'

Forty-five minutes later, Angel heard the doorbell go, and Ruth rushed in to kiss Angel goodbye and told her to call the minute she finished at St Ted's that evening to tell her all about it. Checking her phone, Angel calculated that she had about twenty minutes' more time to study, then she'd shower and, even factoring in the ten-minute bus ride over to St Ted's, she'd still be there well in time for the ten o' clock start . . .

Angel felt her eyes snap open with a start as her phone beeped with a message. *Wait, why were my eyes closed?* Disoriented, Angel felt around among her rumpled bedclothes for her phone, and saw Izzy's message.

Keep your eye out for sexy docs to make Caspar jealous with!

Angel ignored the message, but instead stared at the time on her screen. Nine fifteen. She hadn't even showered yet! Snatching off her silk bonnet, she leapt out of bed and ran to the shower. How had she managed to fall asleep and end up late again? Maybe Caspar's bad habits were starting to rub off on her? It didn't matter now – what *did* matter was trying to get to the hospital even vaguely on time!

Her lungs felt like they were on a sizzling barbeque fuelled by her own stupidity as Angel legged it for the bus which was idling at the stop with its indicator already signalling a move out into the traffic.

'Wait!' she shouted, feeling a tiny grain of relief as an elderly man took his sweet time after the driver had opened the door for him, allowing Angel to pound along the pavement up to the bus and swing herself up inside just as the driver finally pulled away.

'Tha . . . Thank you,' she wheezed, at nobody

in particular. She flopped, thirsty and agitated, into the nearest seat, ignoring the disapproving look of the middle-aged woman next to her who had seemed to think her handbag needed its own special resting place. Once her pulse began to return to normal, Angel risked glancing at her phone. It was exactly eight minutes to ten, and the bus was sitting in traffic. *Fantastic*. When she'd scratched to reveal today's message on her advent calendar earlier that morning, it had said something about exercising patience. She'd found the patients/patience coincidence cute at the time, but now Angel was just irritated. It was as if the universe was mocking her.

As she stared at her phone screen wishing time would stand still, Angel saw a familiar name pop up above a message coming through on her screen. Caspar? In spite of everything, she felt a fizz and an excited, relieved smile at the sight of it. But her mood plummeted again as she saw what he'd written.

Hey Angel. Really sorry but not sure I'm gonna be able to keep working with you on fundraising. Need more time freed up after school. Not to do with what we said last night. I want to make it up to you/explain, if you can meet up?

Great. So not only was she late because of worrying about all the Caspar business, possibly messing up her big opportunity to get something under her belt that could genuinely impress Dunstable Academy, but now he was abandoning her completely? She should have seen this coming, really. He was probably freeing up time to spend with Tilda. Angel knew it was silly, but she had to swallow back tears, and she almost missed her stop for the hospital as she re-read his message.

As she got off the bus, she typed back:

Fine. It'll probably be easier working with someone else anyway. And I'm busy atm. Can't meet.

As she walked through the sliding doors of St Ted's Hospital, Angel deliberately turned off her phone. She'd had enough of all this drama with Caspar, she tried to tell herself, feeling a mixture of anger, disappointment and real sadness. She should have known not to trust him again. And she knew that for now, she needed to concentrate on the course.

She stared at the map of the hospital in the foyer, and then finally managed to find her way through the maze of departments, frequently being told by nurses not to run, until she arrived where she had been told to go. A gathering of seven or eight students around her age were holding their notebooks and nodding excitedly, already all dressed in white coats. Angel dropped her backpack breathlessly at her feet and scrabbled to dig her notebook out. Dr Benedict was standing in her own white lab coat by the reception desk in the department, speaking to everyone. 'Oh, Angel Green. Lovely to see you, thanks for joining us,' she said, smiling at Angel.

'S-sorry I'm late,' Angel said, feeling everyone's eyes on her. Of course they were all perfect, they'd never be late or have a shambles of emotions raging inside them, or have thrown on the clothes nearest the door ... Angel suddenly wondered if this was how Caspar felt sometimes. Then she remembered that a) she wasn't thinking about him any more and b) he'd somehow style this out a lot better than she was, currently.

'No problem at all,' Dr Benedict said. 'I'm just outlining what we'll be doing today. We'll split you into smaller groups, and you'll all shadow me and a couple of my colleagues as we go round and see some of our patients. We'll show you how we record our findings and decide on any medications issued. Then we'll get to the good stuff – like observing a surgery! *And* you might even get a chance to do some diagnosis, and be put into a stimulated emergency situation to see how you might fare. Sound good?'

Angel nodded emphatically alongside her fellow students, trying hard to focus on what actually sounded like a really exciting day. She tied her braids back and took a deep breath. *You can do this,* she told herself. A girl called Baharati seemed to take pity on Angel as she looked around, confused as the others started to disperse.

'Quick, stash your bag in a locker in there,' the girl said, gesturing to a small room while Dr Benedict turned away to speak to a nurse. 'Your name will have been assigned to one, and there should be a coat in there for you to put on.'

Angel smiled gratefully and hurried in, finding her locker, leaving her bag and grabbing the lab coat inside it. It was a bit big, but it still gave her a rush as she pulled it on and caught a glimpse of herself in the small mirror in the room.

She hustled quickly out again, smiling. Ready.

After all pulling on surgical caps (Angel chose an extra-large one and twisted her braids up into it, relieved that they fit in there), they all gathered around as a real-life, *actual* surgeon did a suturing demonstration on an *actual* real-life patient!

The man was in his twenties, and had a large laceration on his hand from an unfortunate attempt to remove the stone from an avocado. He grinned sheepishly at the gathered students, clearly nicely numbed as they watched the doctor carefully sew the wound back together. Angel was too intrigued to feel queasy, though she had to admit that when they were then all guided to a lab to try suturing for themselves on a side of raw pork (skin on!), she required a few deep breaths, and vaguely considered going vegan like Ola. But only for a second. Concentrating to get the stitches right, Angel felt more at home than she had felt since . . . *No, no, no.* Somehow her mind had floated back to the oddly cathartic, comfortable yet spark-filled after-school moments in the art room with . . .

Not allowed to think his name, she told herself, instead finishing up her sutures and managing a smile as Dr Benedict came over to take a look.

'Wonderful job, Angel. You're a natural,' she said, and Angel's smile turned to a beam. This was what she was meant to do, she could feel it. In spite of whatever might be annoying her outside of the walls of the hospital, and the rocky start arriving embarrassingly late, Angel felt that things were actually going well.

CHAPTER 16

She had thought too soon, though. Of course.

Angel had used all her strength not to turn on her phone at lunchtime, when they all broke out into the canteen to grab something to eat. She could feel the muscles of her fellow students palpably relax the moment they got their phones in their hands. Angel understood the feeling – she was *dying* to look at hers, but she was afraid of what she might see in return from Caspar after her stern message this morning. Or . . . not see. Would that be worse? She wasn't sure. But when they stopped for a short afternoon break before their final tasks, Angel was able to resist no longer. As they all rushed to their lockers again to grab and check their phones, she followed suit, turning hers on and waiting as it came to life.

There was a message from her mum, of course, asking how things were going, saying it was nice down in Brighton (Angel felt her jaw clench a bit at the photos of the seafront, and of Victor and his daughter beaming in front of some painting she'd apparently done). Angel replied quickly that things were going well. There were a couple in the group chat that she, Izzy and Ola had, with the girls saying they were coming over tonight, and then descending into a lengthy interaction between her friends about what flavour of ice cream was best. She quickly replied that she'd see them later.

And then there was one from Caspar. All it said in reply to her saying she was happy to work with someone else, and that she couldn't meet up with him, was:

I'm sorry to hear that.

Angel wasn't sure what she had expected. The whole idea that something might have been brewing between the two of them now seemed totally absurd and embarrassing. She tried to stuff down the disappointment, ignoring his message and quickly glugging a can of cola before they were called back to the lab room.

For their final task, Angel and her fellow students were asked to apply some of what they'd learned over the course of the day in an imaginary drill in the Accident & Emergency department. Angel, feeling confident, raised her hand when Dr Benedict asked who wanted to go first.

'Fantastic, Angel, thank you. So, let's see who's come in for you,' Dr Benedict said, fanning out a number of envelopes and holding them out towards Angel. She took one, and opened the envelope eagerly.

'It's number four,' Angel read out loud. 'A thirty-seven-year-old man presenting with a severe head wound having fallen off a ladder.' Her reading slowed as she studied the card. Potential brain injury, like her dad. It wasn't quite the same, but her father had been at a roofing job, which he did all the time, when he'd had the brain haemorrhage. It was only his colleague's quick reaction that had stopped him toppling off. But an undiagnosed condition had taken him anyway. There was nothing that could have been done – Angel still remembered the doctor coming to tell her and her mum that. Angel's heart began to race. *Not now, don't panic.*

Angel watched as Dr Benedict gestured through the glass window into the corridor at a group of people gathered outside their lab room. Her heart began to pump even harder as a black man was wheeled in on a stretcher, with what Angel assumed was fake – but surprisingly realistic – blood on his head, groaning.

Please, just don't panic, Angel told herself.

'Tell us what you'd do first,' Dr Benedict was asking. Angel swallowed hard, but managed to run through the protocols they'd been taught over the course of the day, hugely anxious as Dr Benedict was now taking notes rather than giving them indications of whether they were right or wrong. Angel thought she'd got through it all correctly, but she was breathing hard, trying to remember each of the stages. When she finished, she studied Dr Benedict's face, feeling the blood drain away from her own as she realised the doctor looked faintly disappointed.

'OK, good job in general, Angel,' she began, 'but there were a few things you missed, I'm afraid. Some of them were minor – remember we always glove up first thing, but a nurse would have handed you the gloves so that's not too serious.' She paused. 'But the key thing was failing to ask if your patient was allergic to penicillin, as is standard. So if your patient here shows you his info card . . .' The man, who Angel now recognised as part of the local am-dram society, pulled a sympathetic face as he handed Angel the information card he and his fellow actors had clearly each been given. Angel read the notes, horrified.

'Penicillin allergy,' she whispered.

Dr Benedict took a step closer and placed a comforting arm on Angel's shoulder. 'Which would result in?' she asked gently.

'Anaphylactic reaction. Possibly even death,' Angel murmured, still in shock. She knew it was all pretend, of course, but how could she have overlooked something that had the potential to be so serious for her patient? She felt hot prickles of tears suddenly threaten in her eyes, and swallowed hard. What if she wasn't cut out to be a doctor after all? What then?

'Now, that's why we run drills like this. We do it even after you've started studying properly,' Dr Benedict said, aiming her words at Angel and the rest of the students. 'This is just a day-long taster course. Angel, remember you've learned a huge amount in a short space of time, so you should be very proud. And I doubt you'll be forgetting the penicillin enquiry again any time soon, right?' She smiled encouragingly.

Angel nodded, still not trusting herself to speak.

'Now, who's next?'

Angel hadn't expected to feel relieved that the course was over. The excitement she'd felt earlier in the day when things were going well had melted into a puddle of self-pity, and it took everything she had to sound bright to her mum on the phone as she trudged back to the bus stop in the cold.

'Yeah, it went well,' Angel said, channelling her perkiest self. 'Thanks so much for arranging it with Dr Benedict, Mum. It was amazing!'

'Well, good, I'm glad,' her mum said, but then Angel heard someone calling her name in the background. 'Yes, darling, I'll be right with you,' she heard her mum reply. Then her voice got louder again. 'We're just heading down to the gallery again for the evening event. I'll send you a photo. I'm wearing that other dress you helped me choose. Anyway, Angelface, be good, and we'll speak later, and in the morning, yeah?'

'Yeah,' Angel replied. She said goodbye to her mum, but in that moment, she felt really far away from her, and the thought made her even more down in the dumps. A freezing drizzle began while she waited for the bus back home, which Angel thought was about right.

Still, things picked up at least a tiny bit when, an hour after she got home, the doorbell rang and Izzy and Ola barrelled in as she answered it. And a tiny bit more when she saw what Ola whipped out of her giant backpack (after pulling out a seemingly endless, unravelled and puffy sleeping bag). Her games console!

They ordered way too much pizza, and Angel regaled her friends with her tale of woe from the course – as well as the awkward and then mysterious stuff with Caspar the night before. They studied every syllable of his text messages, and Angel's reply.

'This is totally fixable,' Ola said confidently, chewing a pizza crust. 'You just have to play it cool.'

'I think basically telling him to get lost is colder than cool, O,' Angel said. Part of her wanted to just draw a line under the whole affair. She flipped her braids away from her face and sat up straighter.

'Do you know what? Let's forget about boys for tonight. Including the old men trying to get in with our parents,' she said, thinking about her mum being pulled away from her by *Victor darling* and his silly family.

'And the creepy stepmums growing humans inside them *just* to spite us!' Izzy joined in.

'And the . . . Actually, I'm good,' Ola said, and they all laughed. 'Come on, it's time for me to kick your butts at *Just Dance!*'

They hooked up the games console, and were soon arguing about who was going to dance to which songs. Angel grinned at her friends. At least they could be relied on to help make things better!

Angel's one act of rebellion for the night was to enlist their help in dragging her mattress down from her bed so they could all sleep downstairs on the floor of the living room watching late-night TV and telling each other ghost stories. Inevitably, that ended in all three of them huddling together on the mattress, convinced that a mask-wearing maniac was trying to break in through the kitchen window.

Eventually, though, Izzy and Ola drifted off to sleep. As she listened to her friends' soft snores, Angel sneaked a final look at her phone. Should she message Caspar to apologise? No. She had a better idea. Finally feeling better all around, she settled down to get some sleep herself.

CHAPTER 17

Sunday 14th December

'I'm barely able to walk on my two feet, let alone skate, O,' Izzy was complaining, slurping on the tea that Angel had made them the next morning. But Ola was relentless.

'You need to get into a mind-over-matter state one of these days, Izz. I mean, how can we have that incredible ice rink set up every year, the most Christmassy thing you can possibly imagine, and yet you continue to refuse to set foot – or skate – on it? It's madness! Angel, help me out here. We're going skating this morning, yes?'

'I'll just watch,' Izzy whined, but Ola sprang up from the kitchen table and pulled Izzy with her. Angel mopped up the spilled tea, laughing as Izzy screwed up her face. Ola took her into a dance hold and pretended to glide her around the living room, leaping over the games controllers and bedclothes strewn all around it.

'Imagine the wind in your hair!'

'I'm imagining you two knocking over the TV,' Angel said. 'But totally, we're going.' She held up a hand as Izzy was breathlessly allowed to come to a halt and started to protest again. 'All of us, definitely on the ice. But first, we're clearing things up here before Mum gets back. And,' she said in more of a mumble, 'I need to pop down to the high street to pick something up, but then I'll meet you guys at the rink.'

'Très mysterious-o,' Izzy said, landing back in her chair at the kitchen table and spooning some of the terrifyingly mulchy cereal she had left in her bowl into her mouth. Apparently it tasted better that way. 'But fine, we'll clear up, Ola and I will go and dump our stuff home, and then I'll meet you guys to observe this skating malarkey at elevenish, then we'll go and grab a sandwich at the Crafty Cuppa, where I may or may not have it on good intel that a certain Patel brother could be hanging out, and that'll be cool! Great, let's get to it.'

She moved her bowl to the sink and started vigorously washing up the stuff they'd left in there. Angel and Ola exchanged looks, then both said at the same time, 'You're definitely skating!'

An hour later, her friends had left to go and get ready for the skating excursion, and Angel had showered and dug around for all the loose bits of change she could find. She scratched off the day on her calendar to reveal the next challenge before she headed out.

Work hard. Stay humble.

It was a weird one, she thought, but wildly appropriate for her plans before meeting back up with Ola and Izzy. Heading down the high street in the bright, cold sunshine, Angel hesitated only a moment as she stood outside the art supply-cum-haberdashery shop. She was relieved to find the item she wanted to purchase was just about within her budget, and bought it before she could change her mind.

Walking back towards the rink, Angel was debating whether she should package up the gift she'd just bought and leave it on her intended recipient's doorstep – or whether that was weird, or dramatic, or sent the wrong message – when she saw the person who she'd bought it for. Caspar, of course. And he was heading towards the hospice, *again!* This time, Angel couldn't let it go.

Caspar had headphones on over his knitted hat, and was walking fast with his hands in his pockets towards Angel. He didn't seem to have noticed her yet, so she jogged the last few steps to meet him at the top of the walkway down into the hospice.

'Hey!' she said, then realised he wouldn't be able to hear her. Caspar's hazel eyes seemed to light up for a moment as he saw her, but then quickly darkened again. He slowed reluctantly and lifted one of the earpieces up and behind his ear.

'Angel,' he said. 'Hey.'

She looked down at the pavement, flexing her fingers around the paper bag she had in one hand. 'Listen, I'm ... I didn't mean to sound ... My reply to you yesterday ...'

'Don't worry about it,' Caspar said, his voice unusually hard. 'I'm sorry, too.'

'I know, but it was rubbish of me to be so short with you, and not give you a chance to explain what's going on with you. I genuinely couldn't meet up, though. I had this one-day course at St Ted's, like a taster thing for aspiring doctors.'

Caspar pushed his hands further into his pockets, but his eyes met hers, and for a second he looked interested. 'Cool,' he said finally.

Angel drew a breath. *Be humble,* she thought to herself, like a mantra. 'I really want to hear whatever it is you wanted to tell me, Caspar. I know we could just leave it where it is, but I . . . I don't want us to not be friends again. So?'

Caspar exhaled hard, and a big cloud of condensation lingered in front of his face for a moment. 'I don't want that either. I've missed you,' he mumbled. 'It's probably easier if you come with me.' He gestured towards the hospice.

Angel wanted to ask more questions, but instead she followed Caspar into the familiar environment of the lobby. Evan, one of the nurses who worked with her mum, waved at Caspar as they got closer to the reception desk.

'She's just finishing up with her infusion,' Evan said to him, and then seemed to stop short as he noticed Angel was there. 'Oh . . . Hi, Angel. Your mum's not on today, is she?'

'She's with me, today, Evan,' Caspar said, pushing his earphones down around his neck and pulling off his hat.

'Oh, OK,' the nurse replied, but Caspar was already striding away down a hallway. Angel quickly followed after him again, stopping beside him as he paused next to a room. He knocked softly then pushed the door open. Angel was familiar with the rooms on the wards of the hospice, with their slightly shabby but bright yellow walls, their medical beds and tables and chairs set up by the windows. There was a nurse unhooking a hanging IV from a tiny figure in the bed. It was little girl with warm brown skin and dark hair braided into two pigtails, who beamed when she saw Caspar come into the room.

'Cas!'

'Ruby Roo!' he responded, walking over to give the girl a hug. 'I've brought a friend today, is that cool?'

The girl smirked and looked from Caspar to Angel and back again. 'A *girl* friend?'

Caspar mock-frowned, though Angel could tell he was a bit embarrassed. 'Ruby, this is Angel.' He turned. Angel swallowed, already unexpectedly touched at what she was watching, and confused, and happy and . . . all her feelings were vying with each other.

'Angel,' Caspar said. 'This is my sister, Ruby.'

CHAPTER 18

'Go . . . shay disease?' Angel repeated tentatively. She and Caspar had pulled the two small armchairs in the room up closer to Ruby's bed, and she seemed to be enjoying having a captive audience.

'Yes, Gaucher Disease,' said Casper. 'Sounds fancy, doesn't it?

'I've had it since I was born, haven't I, Cas?' Ruby said with a smile.

Caspar nodded, and Angel noticed how proudly he was watching his sister. They had the same smile, the same warm brown skin tone and hazel eyes. 'It basically means Rubes has an enzyme disorder that affects her liver, spleen, bone marrow . . . Her bones can fracture easily, hence this bad boy.' He gestured to a cast on Ruby's leg, which was propped up on a pillow. 'She fell and broke her leg again on the day of the first screening.'

Angel wasn't sure what to say. She felt terrible for how annoyed she'd been about Caspar not turning up that day. This explained so much of his behaviour. She'd had the vague knowledge that Caspar's sister had some health issues, but it felt so strange that his six-year-old sister, and his family, had been going through all of this and she'd been in some oblivious bubble. It hurt that her mum hadn't mentioned anything, even though she knew that Ruth had to keep her patients' confidentiality.

'It's from my mummy's side of the family,' Ruby said, with a glance to Caspar for his approval before chuckling. It seemed like something she must have heard them talk about before, but Angel marvelled at how mature she sounded. Having been through so much, it seemed inevitable Ruby would have had to grow up fast.

Caspar turned to Angel, his eyes shy and earnest. 'Rubes has enzyme infusions every two weeks. She's been having some tough days lately so we've had to bring her into the hospice a bit more than we usually would,' he explained. 'And my parents' accountancy business has been under a lot of pressure too, so I wanted to be here more for Rubes, and to help them out. I'm sorry it meant I had to step back from the fundraising, Angel. I honestly have loved working with you, and it meant more than you could know that we were raising money for this place. It's really special – everyone here, especially your mum, has been amazing. Haven't they, Ruby-Roo? Nurse Ruth is Angel's mum!'

'Nurse Ruth!' Ruby exclaimed excitedly. 'She's the best!'

'She is, isn't she?' Angel replied, smiling but feeling tears burning in her eyes as well. Ruby became distracted by the TV she had turned on in the corner – apparently it was time for her favourite cartoon – and so Angel turned to Caspar, her voice low. 'Caspar . . . I am so sorry. I feel terrible for being so hard on you when all this was going on. It's actually amazing that you've been balancing everything. You're an amazing brother, and I'm an . . . an idiot.'

Angel's mouth went dry as Caspar reached over and touched her hand as it rested on the arm of the chair. 'You're not an idiot, Angel,' he said with a laugh. His hand remained on hers, and his eyes drifted down to where they connected, like he was a bit surprised to see them like that. He waited a moment longer, silent, before gently moving it away. 'It's a relief to have this all out in the open. I'm not sure why, but I was worried that if lots of people knew about what Ruby was going through—'

'And what you're dealing with, too,' Angel interrupted.

'Yeah. I just didn't want people feeling sorry for us, or asking loads of questions, or . . . There's more to Rubes than her illness, you know? I don't know. It seems stupid now. Especially with you. I . . . I trust you.'

Their eyes connected, and Angel felt a rush of something really strange, but fizzy and exciting.

'Angellll?' Ruby said in a sing-song voice, and they both jumped and turned to Ruby again. She was proffering a marker pen. 'Will you write on my cast?' Angel quickly obliged and then Ruby said, 'Hey, and Cas, you said that today we could go for a walk before it gets dark? Or more like a roll, for me!' She burst into fits of contagious giggles at her joke, pointing at the wheelchair in the corner.

'That's right, I did,' Caspar said, chuckling too. 'Angel, do you want to come?'

Angel suddenly remembered. 'Whoops! I'm actually meant to be meeting Izzy and Ola over at the ice rink right now! Shall we head that way, would that be OK?'

'Yes, yes, yes!' Ruby shouted. 'I want to go to the ice rink. Please, Cas?'

Caspar hesitated. Angel suspected that even though he'd opened up to her, he wasn't totally comfortable with other kids at school knowing about Ruby.

'Go on,' she told him. 'It will be fun.'

Caspar smiled and nodded. 'No fair – two against one. Ruby loves skating, when she's well enough. She loves all kinds of sport, actually, right, Rubes?' He looked at Angel. 'She and Josh talk each other's ears off about football.'

It felt like Angel was having a whole new side of Caspar's life opened up to her, and she was really glad that he had a friend like Josh who clearly knew what he had going on and was supportive, too. They OKed the excursion with Nurse Evan, and then got Ruby into some warmer clothes and into her wheelchair to head out towards the rink. It was only as she gathered her stuff that Angel remembered she hadn't yet given Caspar the present she'd bought him. She decided to wait until later, already a bit embarrassed, and stuffed it into her bag.

'Uh, what time d'you call—' Izzy began as she saw Angel approaching at the entrance to the rink. But as she saw who Angel had in tow, she stopped short and broke out into a massive grin. 'Who do we have here?' she said. 'Hey, Caspar.'

'Hey, Izz,' he said, then nodded at Ola. 'Hey, Ola. This is my sister, Ruby.'

'Hiya!' Ruby said, waving enthusiastically up at Angel's friends with mittened hands.

Angel leaned down to Ruby. 'We have a special mission today, Ruby,' she said conspiratorially, winking at Ola. 'And it's to get Izzy here out on to the ice!'

Ola held up three pairs of skates, but Izzy was already shaking her head. 'I think I've changed my mind . . .' she began, but Ruby clapped, giggling.

'Yes, you have to go skating!' she cried.

'You can't deny a little girl like this,' Caspar said, pinching Ruby's cheek. She squirmed away. 'In fact, Ruby and I are going to get out on the ice as well.'

'Really?' Ruby said eagerly. 'We can do the wheelchair skating again?'

'Yup!'

Ruby cheered, and Caspar went off to hire his own skates. Angel wheeled her over to the benches and she, Ola and a reluctant Izzy laced up their skates, standing up and wobbling.

'So, things have taken a turn for the better with . . .' Izzy murmured, nodding to where Caspar was heading back over to them, expertly balancing on his skate blades on the rubber flooring.

'Yeah,' Angel whispered, blushing a bit, 'I suppose they have.'

A few moments later, Izzy was clinging to the side of the rink and shrieking in a mixture of terror and laughter, Ola was zipping in near-professional circles and intermittently mocking her, and Angel was just about holding her own between the two of them. She skated over to the entrance to the rink, frowning as she saw what Caspar was up to. He wheeled his sister over, hoisted her wheels up, and before Angel knew it, he'd pushed her right out on to the ice! There wasn't the same kind of traction as on the ground, so her wheels slid along the surface. Ruby whooped in delight, and although one or two of the attendants looked a little dubious, they didn't stop Caspar. Who could resist the sweet little girl who lit up as he swooped her around the rink? A few people broke out in applause, and Angel joined in.

'Brilliant!' she called to them as Caspar let go of his sister's chair and skated backwards around her while she laughed and clapped. He was really good – of course. Angel skated over, wobbling as she reached Caspar and Ruby, and he reached out to take her hand and steady her. He wordlessly massaged her cold fingers in his gloved ones for a moment before letting go.

'This is so cool,' she said, nodding down at Ruby as they skated along behind her while Caspar pushed. 'I'm wondering ... how many other patients at the hospital do you think might be able to come out here on the ice?'

'In wheelchairs and stuff?' Caspar enquired, looking over at her. 'Hmm ... I don't know, six or seven of them, maybe? Just a guess, though. Why, what are you thinking?'

'I'm not a hundred per cent sure yet . . .' Angel replied.

A few moments later, she was swept up in a three-person chain with Ola and Izzy, who all screeched and laughed as Izzy's lack of coordination sent them sprawling across the ice. Caspar skated over to help them all up, grinning.

'I'm well and truly done with this sliding on ice malarkey,' Izzy declared, hobbling off and sighing exaggeratedly as she landed back on the rubber surrounding the rink. She quickly began unlacing her skates.

'I'd better be getting this one back to the hospice, too,' Caspar said.

Angel nodded, and pulled her phone out of her bag. 'Yeah I think Mum's going to be home soon, so I should probably head off, too. I'll walk you guys back there, though.'

Ola and Izzy tactfully hung back as Angel said goodbye and headed off towards the hospice with

Caspar and Ruby, who was chattering excitedly about how much fun she'd had, and how much she liked Angel's friends. They got Ruby safely situated back in her room, where Caspar and Ruby's parents were waiting.

'Angel Green! Well I never!' Oscar Johnson, Caspar's father exclaimed, standing up from the chair he'd been sitting in reading a paper. His dark eyes shone beneath his glasses as he grinned at her, looking like an older, slightly darker, almost-as-handsome version of his son. It had been years since Angel had really seen the Johnsons in anything other than passing, but when she reached a hand out to shake his, Mr Johnson batted it away and engulfed her in a bear hug. 'So good to see you, young lady! Oh, gosh look at you.' He sighed and stepped back to look at her. 'I know James would have been so proud of the woman you're becoming.' He shook his head with a mixture of nostalgia and regret. 'We've been asking Ruth all about you.'

'Yes, sweetheart. *So* sorry it's been so long. Your mum is just an absolute godsend, you know,'

Rebecca Johnson added, waiting until her husband released Angel's hands, and then taking her into a hug of her own. Angel felt a bit overwhelmed, but she smiled at the petite woman, whose loose dark curls were now streaked here and there with flecks of grey as they were pulled back into a bushy afro bun.

'So good to see you all,' Angel said, smiling over at Caspar. 'But I'd better be getting home now. So good to meet you, Ruby!'

The little girl had settled back into the bed – Caspar had told Angel that they'd agreed to have her stay one more night before she went home – and now she stretched out her arms for her own hug. Angel obliged happily, realising there was only one Johnson left that she hadn't embraced . . .

'I'll walk you out,' Caspar told her, and they both ignored the look his parents exchanged as they left the room and headed into the corridor, and on towards the sliding doors. As they did, Angel remembered again the gift she'd bought

Caspar. She paused and pulled it out of her backpack, her cheeks burning.

'Erm, I got you this,' she mumbled, not looking quite at him as she held the bag out to Caspar. 'Sort of as an apology or whatever.'

'Really?' he said, taking it. She could feel his quizzical gaze, but then he turned his attention to the gift bag, opening it and pulling out the lino-cutting set.

'I remembered you saying your blades were blunt, and it was really cool doing the lino cuts the other week, and I felt really bad about things, and then obviously meeting Ruby now has just made it ten times worse, but, like, better too, and I just thought you might like it but obviously if it's the wrong kind it was just the art supply shop on the high street, so—'

'Angel?' Caspar said, and she took a breath at last. 'I love it.'

'Are you sure?'

'Absolutely.'

She risked a proper look at him, and he took a

step closer. Angel had never been more grateful that the nurses had been called away from the front desk. Caspar reached over and brushed some stray braids away from her face, then wordlessly pulled her in towards his chest and wrapped his arms around her. Angel's limbs went stiff for a moment, before she melted into Caspar and put her arms around him, too.

'Thank you,' he said, and his voice was a low rumble that moved through her whole body.

'You're welcome,' she whispered.

CHAPTER 19

Monday 15th December

Even this early in the morning on a Monday, there was a definite buzz around the school halls as people began to trickle in. The final week of term – at last! Angel felt smug as she headed into the school council room and found she was the first person there. She felt a buzz of excitement as she opened her notebook to go over her proposal in her head one more time. It involved a little bit of a white lie, but she reckoned it would be forgiven. Her advent calendar this morning had been a bit abstract – apparently she had to:

Light a spark.

But she had a feeling this just might . . .

'Angel Green, bright and early, that's what we like to see,' Tilda said as she strode into the room with Olivia hot on her heels. Angel ignored the patronising tone and smiled at the head of the council – she needed to butter her up. Eventually the rest of the group gathered in the classroom, including Caspar, who made a beeline for the seat next to Angel. She may or may not have balanced her backpack on it to deter anyone else from sitting there. He sat down next to her just as Tilda called the meeting to order, so he reached over and scrawled 'Hey there' on her notebook with a smiley face. It was silly but Angel was a little mortified to find how gooey it made her insides go.

The school disco was highest on the agenda since it was coming up soon, and everyone talked excitedly about the plans for decorating the school hall in a *'Winter is coming'* theme – something about a TV show that Angel had never got into. She had almost forgotten about the disco altogether, seeing as she knew most of her free time that week was going to be dominated by last-minute preparations for the Dunstable Academy entrance exam. But at last, talk turned to the fundraiser, and the final film of the year on Friday.

'So, Angel, Caspar, what are your plans for the last film? Better be a good one!'

Angel cleared her throat, trying not to sound nervous. 'Well, a few things have come up. We haven't had as much time as we'd hoped to plan for the next screening,' she began, and Caspar glanced at her, his expression quizzical. Even though he'd said he had to step back a bit, they'd had a brief discussion about keeping things fairly simple with an assembly announcement of a *Home Alone* screening instead of new posters, and just popping some corn as snacks, which Angel had told him she could take care of. 'But we've actually come up with an even better idea!'

She expected more in the way of a ripple of

gasps, but everyone was still looking a bit too sleepy for that. Everyone, that was, except Tilda, who put her hands on her hips and shook her head.

'We agreed on movie screenings. It's in the minutes.'

Olivia glanced up from her notes. 'Let's hear Angel out,' she said, then her eyes widened as if she hadn't planned to say something out loud.

Angel smiled at her, and gave her a subtle wink. 'Thanks, Olivia. I had been thinking . . . We've got the perfect place to do something really cool right here in our town. The ice rink!'

'Right . . .' Tilda said, sceptical eyebrow raised.

'I say we move the last fundraising event there. My mum knows one of the people who runs it, so I gave her a call last night and she said we could use it for an hour on Friday.' She looked over at Sanj. 'The choir was such a hit the other day. We could have some singing, sell some hot spiced apple juice, and maybe have a stall about the hospice and all the amazing work they do . . .'

She was building up to her biggest idea, and Angel risked a glance at Caspar, who was nodding enthusiastically. 'Actually, I thought we could involve the hospice a bit more in this one. Because what's the best way of getting people to part with their cash for a good cause?'

'What?' Olivia chimed in, egging Angel on.

'*Show them* the community they're helping. Show them what their money would be going towards, the real lives they're affecting. There are a good few people who are cooped up in their rooms at the hospice all day, when we could pretty easily take them out on an excursion to the ice rink. I know it sounds a bit weird, but we can even take them out on the ice to experience a bit of skating for themselves!'

Murmurs rippled around the group, but Angel's heart sank as she saw Tilda shaking her head. 'Sounds like an absolute health and safety nightmare to me,' she said.

'But—' Angel began. But to her surprise, Caspar stood up beside her.

'Actually, it's totally safe. I take my sister Ruby standing sometimes. We did it just yesterday, in fact,' he said, looking at Angel. She fought the urge to squeeze his arm in support, especially when he added, 'And she ... she's actually a patient at the hospice. I'm certain it would be OK with them, for the people who are up to it. As long as they fill out the right forms and stuff. They'd have some hospice volunteers, nurses, people's family members, and we'd all be up for helping out, I'm sure. Right, guys?' Caspar spread a grin around each of the students at the table.

More murmurs rippled around the council members, sounding a little more positive. The Caspar Johnson charm was working on them!

'It seriously makes a difference being able to get out and do something fun,' he continued, 'especially around this time of year. Sometimes people might need hospice care over the Christmas period, and a trip like this would really let them get into the spirit even when they may not be able to spend the big day at home. Those positive moments are lifesavers when things are tough for someone you love, trust me.' He paused, and seemed to battle his emotions for a moment. He took a deep breath. 'Anyway, I personally think it's an amazing idea.' He looked at Angel with a sincerity in his eyes that almost made her well up, too.

Even Tilda seemed quite moved by Caspar's revelation, and his passion for Angel's proposition. 'We'll have to put it to a vote,' she said grudgingly. 'All those in favour of swapping the last event from a film screening to ice skating, raise your hands.'

Everyone lifted a hand in the air, and Angel couldn't help a little laugh as Olivia recorded enthusiastically in her notes.

'Amazing. Thanks so much, guys. It's going to be brilliant,' she said. Soon afterwards they wrapped things up, the bell went and they all began to bundle out of the room towards their classes. Angel hung back, pulling Caspar to one side. 'I hadn't meant for you to have to tell everyone about Ruby or anything . . .'

'No, it's incredible, Angel. And I think it was time to let everyone know about it. I don't know why I was holding on to it for so long. You showed me that people will be cool – really kind, even – about it. And if they're not, well . . . They can get lost, basically!'

Angel nodded, then looked down at her shoes as she felt Caspar's gaze settle on her. After a couple of moments she looked up, and he was still looking at her, standing close. 'Hey,' she said quietly, 'are you sure you're OK?'

Caspar exaggeratedly straightened his school tie like he was brazening things out, but then he shrugged. 'It's a pretty emotional subject.' They both looked towards the door as the second bell went. 'Better get going,' he said, watching her a moment longer before giving her his signature wink and strolling out of the door.

As Angel emerged from the classroom where they'd had the council meeting, she ran into Izzy on the way to class. 'How's it going? Did they like that idea you told me about last night?' she asked.

'Yeah, it went really well,' Angel murmured, watching Caspar's back as he headed down the hallway ahead of them. Izzy followed her gaze, then hooked her arm into Angel's.

'Come on, I'd better guide you to maths, seeing as you have those heart eyes crowding your vision!'

Angel wasted no time heading straight home after school that afternoon, already running through the revision notes she had recorded on her phone as she walked home. Izzy, Ola and a couple of the other girls had decided to get the bus to go Christmas shopping in the next town, but much as it pained Angel not to be able to go with them, the pressure was starting to really push down on her about the Dunstable Academy entrance exam. She didn't think she'd ever been as nervous about anything in her whole life.

When she got home, she felt a pang of sadness

that the house was quiet – as usual, her mum was already out at work at the hospice for the evening. Angel had hardly had a chance to catch up with her the evening before when she had returned home from Brighton, as she had apparently been 'really knackered'. She almost felt like she and her mother were living completely separate lives at the moment. But as she headed into the kitchen, Angel felt a familiar warmth as she saw that her mum had left a pot on the stove and a note on the table. She'd made her famous peanut butter stew! All Angel had to do was cook some rice and she had a delicious mum-cooked dinner.

'OK, winning parent points there,' Angel said to herself with a chuckle. She went upstairs to change into her comfies, and then put the rice on to cook. As she started to pull her books out of her backpack to spread around the kitchen table, a package wrapped in now-familiar paper fell out of her bag. Angel turned the tag over with a big smile.

To keep you snug on the ice.
Love, Secret Santa

She unwrapped the soft package, and unveiled
– a pair of fuzzy, woolly socks! They were even
yellow, her favourite colour. *Was* Mum her Secret
Santa? *She must be feeling* really *guilty about going
off with Victor,* Angel thought. But deep down she
knew it couldn't really be her mother giving her all
these amazing presents. She knew Ruth found it
hard enough to come up with the money for gifts
on Christmas day, as well as their Christmas dinner;
she wouldn't spend more just to mess about with
Angel for her Secret Santa. It had to be Izzy or Ola.

She typed a message into their group chat:

Come clean, you guys. One of you two is getting
me these Secret Santa gifts, aren't you?

She sent a selfie while holding up the pair of socks
while pulling a silly face.

Ola replied first.

Def not me! But those are extra cute!!

Izzy replied a moment later, with a video of her shaking her head with her hand on her heart.

Then Angel could see she was sending a voice message – because she could never fit just a short reply into their chats!

'By the way, we swung through the fair after we came back from the shops in Rexborough, and I'm sure I saw a stall selling a few advent calendars like yours. Or, similar ones anyway, like all hand made. But they just said 'Christmas Wishes'. I thought about getting one for my little sister but then I was like, it's already halfway through December and she'd complain about there being no chocs in it, which is fair enough to be honest—'

The message stopped abruptly and Angel chuckled – Izzy had clearly run out of space.

Oh cool. Anyway, better get back to these.

Angel snapped a picture of her books laid out on the table, then signed off. Even if her friends said it wasn't them who had been buying her the Secret Santa gifts, she thought slipping the socks on and wiggling her toes in the cosy wool, these *would* be perfect for their day on the ice!

After eating her tasty dinner, Angel was on a roll with her studying when another message came through on her phone.

Time to reconvene the decorating committee. Idea: Bluebells.

Angel smiled as she saw it was from Caspar and typed her reply:

Bluebells?

Yes. For Bluebell Hospice? Keep up, AG!

Angel chuckled and typed back:

You're going to have to elaborate.

You, me, art room, lunchtime tomorrow. All will be apparent. x

For what felt like an eternity, Angel stared at the 'x' he'd finished his message with. She was seconds away from messaging Izzy to ask what it might mean, whether it might have been a mistake, and agonising over whether she should use one too. But she decided to bite the bullet – her advent calendar had been challenging her to move outside her comfort zone, and so Angel decided that this was her chance. OK, it was only a small thing, but it was a big deal to her. Taking a deep breath, Angel typed back:

Intriguing! See you then x

She swallowed hard, grinning madly to herself as she turned back to her books. Bring on tomorrow!

CHAPTER 20

Tuesday 16th December

Angel growled under her breath as she angled her little mirror on her desk and tried again, but her hand slipped once more.

'This is why I don't wear makeup,' she said, wiping away the smudged eyeliner as her mum brought in her cup of tea in her Mariah mug.

'Don't poke your eye out!' Ruth said, looking amused.

'Not helpful.'

'Well, might I suggest sharpening it?' her mum said, rummaging in the pencil case sitting nearby. 'What's the occasion anyway? I feel like I should be telling you not to put slap on or something. That's what we mums are meant to do, right?'

Angel rolled her eyes, but took the sharpener quickly. It did help, to be fair. She blinked at herself in the mirror. 'No occasion really . . .' she hedged, and was grateful when her mum let it drop with a knowing smile.

'OK. By the way, the hospice is buzzing with the idea of your ice-skating excursion on Friday,' she said. 'The patients are really excited. It's a lovely thing you're doing. Just when I thought I couldn't be any prouder!' She stood behind Angel and smoothed her daughter's braids around her shoulders, then leaned over to kiss Angel's forehead. Angel screwed up her face, but was proud too.

'Thanks, Mum.'

But as she was leaving the room, Ruth added, 'I think Victor's going to come along, too, on Friday! We can use all the help we can get, right?'

Angel fought not to pull another, more irritated face as she mumbled, 'Yeah, sure.' She knew she had to make more of an effort not to get annoyed again about the whole Victor situation – and frankly, nothing was likely to dampen her mood today.

Angel practically floated through her lessens up to lunch, ignoring Izzy's light teasing about her eyes looking gigantic today, and sniffing around her exaggeratedly, asking whether she was wearing a new perfume. But when it came time for her to head to the arts room at lunchtime, Angel suddenly started feeling a weird butterflies-in-the-stomach sensation.

'Ah-hah!' Caspar said as she pushed the door open. He spread his arms wide with a flourish, and Angel could see that he'd set up a load of card, scissors and other bits and pieces on the long table in the middle of the room. There were also some sandwiches arranged on the lid of a Tupperware box. 'Lunchtime craft mission is go! I got some sarnies since we don't have that much time to crack through these. I seem to remember ham, cheese and pickle was your fave? Hope you've not gone vegan or anything?'

Angel walked over, observing the buffet. She considered teasing him that she had, but she was so touched by the effort that she couldn't bring herself to joke about it. 'I'm super-impressed you remember, to be honest. Yeah.' She picked a sandwich triangle up and took a bite, then gave a joking chef's kiss. 'Delicious!'

'Despite my otherwise complete lack of culinary skills, I could stretch to these,' he said with a laugh, picking one up himself. 'OK, so here's my idea – we make chains of bluebells out of this card, and we can string them up all around the rink for decoration. Should be pretty easy . . .'

'So you say,' Angel said, eyeing his example dubiously.

'Well, you picked up all the other things I've shown you really easily,' Caspar said. She felt a tingle at the compliment. 'Oh, and check this out . . .'

He walked away, and Angel followed him over to where some more pictures were hanging to dry by the sink. She saw a lino cut abstract in vivid blues that she knew immediately was Caspar's work. 'My own little Chagall-inspired piece,' he said, looking at his work with a critical eye.

'It's amazing,' Angel said, sincerely.

Caspar looked a touch bashful. 'Well, having a sharp lino-cutting kit helped,' he said. 'But anyway, enough of that. We've got bluebells to make!'

He showed her how to cut out the card to make a sort of abstract three-dimensional bell shape. At first Angel wasn't sure she'd get the hang of it, but eventually she began to catch up with the frankly impressive rate at which Caspar was churning them out, all between bites of his sandwich.

'Hang on, are those rocket leaves in there?' Angel asked, then laughed as Caspar struggled to chew his food before answering her. 'Serves you right for being greedy,' she said, faux-tutting. 'Anyway, I thought you hated rocket? Remember one time we went round to Josh's house when we were little and his mum made us all eat salad? You were like, "Why does rocket sound so cool if it burns your nose?"' She broke out into laughter at the memory, and Caspar tried to throw a limp, stray leaf at her, which made her laugh even more.

'It's good to see you do that,' Caspar said when she'd recovered.

'What?' she said, finally letting her breath slow.

'Laugh. Sometimes it seems like you're always serious now. I don't know . . .'

Angel wasn't sure what to say – the comment slightly annoyed her. 'What, like I don't have anything to be serious about?' Her mind drifted to all the stuff he and his family had been going through with Ruby and it did make her feel a bit guilty, but the suggestion of a comparison annoyed her a bit. She shrugged in a weak conclusion, focussed on cutting out her card, and heard Caspar draw in a breath as though he was hoping to change the subject.

He nodded at the hairband she'd been given, which was once again holding back her braids. 'So . . . Have you figured out who your Secret Santa is yet?' he asked.

Angel, still a bit distracted, shook her head.

'No . . . I did get some cool socks yesterday, though.'
Suddenly a thought struck her. 'Hang on a minute.'
She thought back to her conversation with Izzy last
night about the calendars. 'I reckon it might be
Josh? I've got him, and actually it makes sense that
he might have got me some of this stuff . . .'

'Josh?' Caspar said, with a flat tone to his voice.

'Maybe? I dunno. He's pretty brainy, sort of
perceptive. It probably wouldn't take too much
digging around to figure out what I'm into, if I've
managed it for him. Well, mostly,' she chuckled.
'Anyway . . .' Angel held up her string of bluebells.
'What do you reckon?'

'Mmm, yeah. Maybe a bit wonky here,' he
pointed to one of them, 'but we'll have loads so
it's all good.'

Angel had to stifle a little bit of a frown. Why
was he being weird again? 'Wow, tough critic
today, eh?' she ventured.

'We're not all *brainy*, but I'm pretty sure I know
my stuff when it comes to crafts . . .' Caspar
mumbled.

Angel was about to ask him why he was being off, but her phone beeped with an incoming message.

Emergency. Oh my gosh. Emergency. Sanj says Manny would be willing to go to the disco with me. Like actually. ARGH!!

Angel laughed as she read the message. 'Wow, Izzy's going to be insufferable,' she said to Caspar as she looked at her screen. 'Manny might be taking her to the disco!'

She picked up her scissors again, determined to get her work right this time, but she looked up as Caspar cleared his throat.

'Um, are you going? To the disco, I mean?' he asked, looking suddenly a bit nervous. He was all over the place today!

'I'm not sure,' Angel said, returning to her careful cutting. 'I mean, Saturday is my entrance exam for Dunstable Academy and that's what I'm mainly focussed on. The disco is usually pretty cringe-worthy, isn't it? I mean, maybe I'll go a bit later and catch up with Izz and Ola, depending on how the exam goes. But it could be that I'll just be rocking in a corner feeling sorry for myself, who knows!' she added, with a wry laugh, even though she genuinely was more nervous about it than she wanted to let on.

'Right . . .' Caspar said. They both exhaled as the bell rang. This lunchtime craft session hadn't quite gone the way Angel had expected it to, but at least they'd made a start on the decorations for Friday. Caspar wasn't saying much as he cleared their stuff away, and Angel wondered if she'd said or done something wrong. Surely he wasn't that annoyed about some poor scissor-work?

'Well, catch you later, Angel,' he said, hoisting his bag on to his shoulder as they exited the art room.

'Yeah,' she said. 'See you.'

She walked away with a puzzled frown on her face.

CHAPTER 21

Izzy's inexplicably enormous bunch of keys jingled loudly as she liberated them from the pocket of her backpack awkwardly. They'd decided to go to hers after school that afternoon, and Angel smothered a smile as her friend exaggeratedly listened at the door for any sign of her stepmother as she unlocked it.

'Ugh,' she said quietly over her shoulder to Angel. 'The monster is in.'

Angel patted her friend on the shoulder sympathetically as they trooped into the hallway of Izzy's house. It was much bigger than Angel's, with an area as you walked in to hang up coats before leading into a large living room, with glass-panelled doors that separated it from the kitchen. There was even a downstairs 'cloakroom' (or toilet as Angel called it), and upstairs they had a whole *four* bedrooms, as well as a big bathroom with a separate shower cubicle! But it never felt to Angel like her friend was anything but envious of Angel's cosy set up – and that was to a large extent due to the difficulties she had with her stepmum, Carol.

'Hi, Mrs Carter,' Angel volunteered. Izzy's stepmother had one eye glued to the television screen, watching one of those programmes where people decide they're moving abroad. She was also browsing the internet on a tablet balanced on her knees, and Angel noticed it was on a page full of little flouncy dresses for babies. One manicured hand rested absently on her tiny baby bump.

'Oh, hello, girls,' she said now as they walked in, smiling to show a row of brilliantly white teeth, in contrast to her tanned skin and blonde ponytail. Izzy murmured a greeting that almost sounded like a growl, and then gave her eight-year-old sister Charly a tickle as she sat cross-legged on the floor, headphones in, playing a game on her own tablet. Angel waved as the girl glanced up with a grin, then followed Izzy as she strode into the kitchen.

'Grab those crisps, babe,' Izzy said, her head already inside the freezer. She dug out two containers of ice cream, setting them on the counter as she rummaged in the cutlery drawer for some spoons.

'Not sure we need two—'

Izzy turned to her with a stern look. 'Did you *see* what I texted you earlier?' she asked. Angel had attempted to talk about the big revelation that Manny might take Izzy to the disco as they walked home, but she had said that they could absolutely not discuss it until they had all the correct snacks and were in the right environment to properly analyse every single aspect of this monumental event.

Angel laughed. 'You're absolutely right,' she

said, mock-seriously. They grabbed the supplies and headed upstairs to Izzy's bedroom. She'd insisted on painting it a rather vibrant shade of violet soon after her dad had announced he and Carol were getting married. He had agreed to it mainly, Angel suspected, so that Izzy might stop sulking for a moment. Now, even though she had confessed to Angel that she actually didn't like it pretty much from the moment it was finished, Izzy refused to admit this to her dad on principle.

They dumped their bags on Izzy's bed, and then assumed their usual position sitting cross-legged on the fluffy round purple carpet in the middle of the floor, with their food in the middle of it. Izzy put on some music, pausing to stand up and give a quick burst of choreography to the Beyoncé live album she had selected. Angel surfed social media on her phone, half-paying attention until she was done.

'One day you'll be glad you were the first to witness my Queen B-esque greatness,' Izzy said breathlessly as she slumped down again, throwing a crisp at Angel, who caught it in her mouth then thrust her fists into the air victoriously. 'Anyway, let's get down to business!'

Izzy spent a good half an hour recreating the situation that had led to her and Ola speaking to Sanj, who had been sitting with Josh at lunch, which had culminated in the apparently offhand but clearly monumental comment from Sanj that he thought Manny would be up for taking Izzy to the dance. They even dialled Ola in for a moment while she was on a break from her after-school acting class.

'I thought Izz was going to spontaneously combust,' Ola said, laughing after they'd got her up on the screen on Izzy's phone.

'So, question is,' Izzy said, 'do I ask Sanj for his brother's number? Do I message him? Do I wait for him to message me? Like, the disco is mere days away. I need to reconfigure all my outfit plans and everything. I mean, we've never really even cared about the disco, and now it's pretty much the most pivotal event of the Christmas social calendar. Who could have expected it?'

'Totally,' Angel murmured. She grabbed her

own phone and quickly typed out a message. 'OK, I've messaged Sanj . . .' She studied her own screen as she saw that he was typing a reply. 'Cool. He's going to get Manny to drop you a message.'

Izzy leapt up.

'Hey!' Angel heard Ola say through Izzy's phone as it went flying.

Izzy grabbed it again. 'Sorry, babe. Oh my gosh. I'd better get off the phone. What if he's trying to ring me or . . . or for some reason I miss the message because . . .' Angel covered her ears as a message flashed up over Ola's face on the screen, and Izzy screeched loudly and high enough for a dog fifty miles away to hear. 'HE. JUST. MESSAGED. ME!'

Happy to tag along with you guys to the shindig on Sat.

It took a full half an hour – during which Ola had to return to her class – in order for Izzy to be talked back down to earth. Manny's message, in a group

Sanj had added them all to, was perhaps not quite the prom-date Izzy was making it out to be, but Angel was still very happy for her friend.

'So what about you, babe?' Izzy asked, then tipped the melted dregs of the pint of ice cream she had put away into her mouth like it was a milkshake. 'We can totally find you *someone*,' she raised any eyebrow, 'to tag along with, too?'

Wow, Angel thought amusedly, *she's already using Manny's vocab!* She noticed that Josh and Caspar were also in the group Sanj had created in the messaging app, and her heart sank a bit.

'Funny you should say that, actually,' Angel said. 'When I was helping Caspar with the decorations for the ice rink at lunchtime, he was asking me about the disco.'

'What do you mean?'

'Well, like if I was going or whatever. But I said that it would depend on how I'm feeling after the Dunstable Academy exam. Then he got all weird on me.'

Izzy stopped with her frankly rather vulgar

licking of the ice cream tub. 'Angel.' She fixed her friend with a look. Angel opened her eyes wide.

'What?'

'He was blatantly asking you to the disco. Hello?'

Angel sat for a moment, thinking. 'You think?'

'Um, yes!' Izzy shook her head.

Angel frowned. 'He was already acting weird after I said that I thought Josh might be my Secret Santa, the way I'm his. Which, by the way, I've totally been neglecting. How many pressies have you got from yours?'

'Two maybe?' Izzy waved her hands in the air to dismiss that. 'That's not the point, Ange! Let's focus on you turning down a date with your dream bae?'

'He's not my . . .' Angel trailed off, still running back over the events of lunchtime. 'I've had quite a few Secret Santa presents, actually. And they're all, like, really thoughtful ones, too . . .'

Something was trying to form in Angel's mind, but she wasn't quite sure what. The calendar, the notes with it . . . *Your face is too pretty to hide* with the hairband which she was still wearing that very moment . . . the mug, the socks . . .

'Why do you think that is?' Izzy said, folding her arms and staring at Angel like she was an idiot. Then she unfolded them to unwrap a chocolate bar and skip a song on her playlist (she'd switched to romantic ballads since Manny's message).

'What do you mean?' Angel asked, though she was starting to realise she had a feeling what her friend meant.

'Angel, babe, for someone so clever you can be really dim. If you can't figure it out by now, I can't be the one to tell you.' Izzy bit into her chocolate emphatically.

'Ca . . . Caspar?' Angel ventured. 'My Secret Santa is Caspar?'

Oh my gosh. OH. MY. GOSH. She was starting to sound like Izzy in her head.

'Duh, hon!'

'But . . .'

'Hmm?'

'How . . .'

'What's that, hon?'

'But the presents have all been so . . .'

'Haven't they just!'

Now that it was in her head, it didn't sound so completely unbelievable. It could be him. It might . . .

'Caspar . . . likes me? Like, *likes me*, likes me?' She struggled with the idea it could be true, but it all made sense now. 'He got me those gifts?' she whispered. 'This is . . .'

'The most romantic thing that's ever happened to any of us?' Izzy said, grinning madly at her. She added, 'And that's saying something, considering the evening I've had.'

'Yes!'

The only problem was, Angel had never had a . . . boyfriend, or a guy interested in her or anything like that. Had she messed things up with Caspar before they'd even begun? And how on earth was she actually going to tell him she'd figured things out?

CHAPTER 22

Thursday 18th December

Angel held the two pence coin in her hand as she stared down at the advent calendar resting beside her bowl of cereal on the breakfast table. She hadn't been able to bring herself to scratch off a circle yesterday either. Ever since she'd figured out that it was almost ninety-nine percent definite that Caspar had been her Secret Santa all along, she was weirdly scared to see the messages he'd written for her on the calendar. Yesterday after school she and her friends had headed back to the stall where Izzy and Ola had seen the other advent calendars being sold, and the vendor had confirmed that '*a young, and may I say gorgeous young man*' had made them for her. He had seen she was giving some of her proceeds to help a children's cancer charity, and said he knew how it was to want to care for young people going through a difficult time. '*We had a lovely conversation, and next thing I knew he'd dropped off ten of these amazing calendars!*'

It had to have been Caspar. Now that she studied her calendar, she could see his talent all over it – the intricacy, the swirling blues of a night-time Christmas sky on its design . . . Angel sighed then got up her courage and scratched off the last two days' worth of wax:

Write down three things you love about yourself.

That was yesterday's message. She wasn't loving too much about herself at the moment, but she resolved to do it in a moment. And today's advent challenge?

Share a problem — it might halve it!

She had plenty of those . . . And she hadn't been able to confront the biggest one yesterday – how to tell Caspar that she'd figured out he was her Secret Santa, and let him know that she fancied him too. Angel wasn't sure if she was disappointed or relieved that the football team had been invited to a special away day and had been gone all of Wednesday. She still had no idea how she was going to speak to Caspar, or even see him, today . . .

Just as she finished scratching off the wax, her mum unlocked the front door – she'd been on a night shift, and looked typically exhausted, but had a big smile for Angel.

'Hiya, sweetheart!' Her smile faded. 'What's up?'

Is it that obvious, Angel wondered? Clearly. 'I just . . .' She glanced at the calendar. It was a bit awkward, but her mum was probably as good as anyone to share her problem with. 'I figured out who my Secret Santa is.'

'And that's a bad thing? It's not that pig-farming boy, is it?' Angel's mum said, taking off her coat and coming to sit down at the table.

Angel managed a chuckle at that. 'It's Caspar.'

Her mum was quiet for a moment, but Angel noticed a small smile forming on her face. 'I had a suspicion,' she said. 'But why's that a bad thing?'

Angel shrugged. 'It's not, I suppose. It's just . . . I think I've messed things up with him, and I don't even know if he actually is into me or I'm reading too much into these gifts, or even how to tell someone I might fancy them, or . . .' She hesitated, glancing at her mum. 'Or really believe someone could fancy me.'

'Angel—' Ruth began, reaching out for her daughter's hand, but Angel cut her off.

'I know, Mum. Like, objectively, I believe I'm a good person, and easy on the eye . . .' She chuckled self-deprecatingly and flipped her braids over her shoulder. 'But nobody's ever really seen me like that. I've always been the brainy girl. I was never the girl that anyone said they were interested in like that.'

Her mum exhaled softly. 'First of all, yes – you are good, gorgeous and the cleverest person I know.' She fixed Angel with a stare. 'Don't let that go to your head.'

Angel pursed her lips in a wry expression.

'But, darling, has it ever occurred to you that Caspar has liked you all this time, and wasn't sure *you* felt the same? Why do you think he'd go to all this trouble otherwise? I'm certain that if he does like you, it's because of your brainy, beautiful self. He might be just as nervous to come out with the truth as you are.'

Angel wanted to dismiss what her mum was saying, but it bizarrely made sense – all these gifts were like he was leading up to something. Had she ruined it all by unintentionally shooting him down when he had asked about the disco?

'I might be brainy, but I think I might also be an idiot,' Angel said, and her mum pushed away from the table.

'Your words not mine, sweetheart!'

'Har har.'

But her mum walked around behind her and gave her a big squeeze of a hug. 'Now, your mother is heading to the shower and then to bed. You, my dear, will figure this all out. If *I* can find new love at my age –' Angel cringed at that idea, but said nothing – 'then you definitely can, too. Night night.' She kissed the top of Angel's head.

'Morning, morning,' she replied.

Before heading off to meet Izzy and walk to school, Angel decided to jot down three things she loved about herself. It felt stupid at first, but as she wrote, it started to make her feel better. In fact, she'd already sort of started when she was talking to her mum:

I love how I feel confident to say I'm intelligent.

I love my beautiful brown skin.

I love that I'm a great friend.

She smiled at her list. How had both the challenges from the advent calendar managed to make her feel better even though she'd been so down in the dumps for the last couple of days? She finished her now-soggy cereal, and gathered her stuff to go and meet Izzy. Today was definitely looking up!

'Ooh, can we stop in the newsagents?' Izzy said as they passed it on the way to school. 'I said I'd pick up a copy of that film mag Ola likes on my way in. You never know, I might become a movie director myself . . .'

It was even colder than it had been for the past few days, so Angel was grateful for even a brief pit-stop in the warmth. They browsed the shelves of magazines, and although it was a bit lacking in imagination, Angel decided to pick up one more Secret Santa gift for Josh – a football magazine she'd seen him looking at before. She rolled it into a tube, then nabbed a rubber band from the lady behind the counter after she and Izzy had paid. She grabbed a piece of paper from her notebook and wrote 'Santa takes a shot!' and tucked it in with the magazine.

'Not exactly Harrods-level gift wrapping, Ange, but it's the thought that counts, eh?' Izzy said with a chuckle as they huddled together to head the rest of the way to school. They had biology class with Josh first thing, so Angel decided to just slip the gift on to the desk where she knew he sat, as they went in. Malcolm Connelly, one of Josh's football teammates – and an annoying one at that – noticed her putting the gift down just as Josh arrived and dumped his bag at his desk.

'Your Secret Santa mystery's busted wide open, Yorke,' Malcolm said, pulling a gross face at Angel.

'Great,' she muttered.

'Ignore him,' Izzy said loudly, shooting eye-daggers in Malcolm's direction.

Josh unfurled the gift with a smile towards Angel, and read the note.

'*Santa takes a shot*?' Malcolm scoffed, reading over Josh's shoulder. 'Takes a shot, eh, Angel?

 302 ♥

Looks like she's got the hots for a certain someone. Come on then, take your shot! Lucky you, Yorkey! I thought she was too stuck up for any of us!'

Angel pursed her lips, wondering why it was today of all days that Ms Larsen had to be late to class. 'Malcolm, why don't you—' she began, but Josh interrupted her.

'First of all, Angel's my mate. Secondly, I don't have this issue, so this is wicked, Ange, thanks! And thirdly I'm taken.'

'Oh yeah?' Malcolm said. People looked around, interestedly. To be honest, even Angel hadn't realised Josh had a—

'Yeah. Sanj Patel,' Josh said. 'Try not to be jealous, though, Connelly.'

Just then, Sanj walked in, and made a beeline for the seat Josh had saved next to him. 'Uh oh, what did I miss?' he asked, sensing the atmosphere.

Angel watched, a grin spreading on her face, as Josh pecked Sanj on the cheek when he sat down. She noticed a blush but also a beam of pride on

Sanj's face. 'Oh, nothing much,' Josh replied, and then let out a long, relieved-sounding sigh with a smile of his own.

'Ah. May. Zing,' Izzy said beside her.

Angel had an even better feeling about today. If Josh could do it, then so could she!

CHAPTER 23

Friday 19th December

Don't panic, Angel repeated to herself as she smoothed cocoa butter into her skin after her shower. *It's going to be totally fine*, she thought as she pulled on her school uniform for the last day of term – and her new fluffy yellow socks for the ice skating later. *Nothing to worry about*, she thought as she washed up her cereal bowl in the sink before heading to meet Izzy on their corner.

She had to wonder why these stressful events had to come in threes. It was bad enough that she had her Dunstable Academy exam tomorrow morning, but she also had the riskiest fundraising event of the year tonight – that was whose crazy idea? Oh yeah, hers. But most of all, she had still not managed to speak to Caspar about her almost-certain Secret Santa theory, and what it might mean for them as friends or . . . something more?

At lunch, Josh informed her that Caspar was off school that day with some kind of bug. Angel looked over the text conversation they'd exchanged when she sent a message to see if he was OK. Somehow it didn't seem right to call or message the fact that she thought he might be her sweet, kind, flirtatious Secret Santa, that she was a fool not to have realised he was trying to ask her out, and that she fancied him too, that is, if he definitely fancied her. So she just said:

Hey, heard you're not feeling well? That sucks! x

OK so at least she'd risked another kiss . . .

He'd replied:

Yeah, I think it's a 24-hour thing, was feeling rubbish when I got back from the football trip last night. But didn't want to risk not being good for the fundraiser tomorrow . . . ;) x

Angel had tried not to obsess over his kiss back. Was that just because she'd put one? But then she'd got distracted by having to head back to class, and had to do more revision after school, so here she was, heading for their final day of term *and* a potentially serious crunch day in terms of her so-called love life . . .

As soon as she reached the corner, Izzy assailed her with a length of silvery tinsel, swooping it around her neck. She already had a matching tinsel scarf balanced above her own proper woolly one.

'*End of terrrrrm!*' she sang.

'Yeah,' Angel replied, not able to muster the same level of enthusiasm.

'Come on, hon. Everything is going to work out fantastically. Especially because it's D-Day for me and Manny tomorrow. I mean, we're mere hours away from the greatest love story – besides you and Caspar the *Handsome* Ghost – that this school has ever known. This whole weekend feels lucky.'

'Well I'm glad you're so confident, Izz,' Angel said. 'Between all of this and my exam tomorrow, to say I'm feeling stressed out is an understatement.'

Izzy linked arms with her and fixed her with a look. 'I've got enough belief in you for the both of us, Ange. Now enough moping. Let's get merry and Christmassy!'

There was definitely a festive atmosphere in the hallways as they made their way to their first class, but Angel knew none of the lessons she had were with Caspar until after lunch. She caught herself doodling his name in her notebook during French, and squiggling love hearts in her margins during geography. She really needed to get a grip!

But just as the bell went for lunch at long last, she was intercepted in the hallway by their headteacher, Mrs Black.

'Ms Green, can you spare a moment of your

lunchtime for me?' she asked, beckoning Angel towards her office with an air that indicated it wasn't actually a request.

Great, Angel thought, *just when I thought this day couldn't get any more stressful* . . . She was pretty sure she hadn't done anything wrong, but to be honest she wouldn't put anything past the universe at the moment.

She headed into the small office with Mrs Black, who moved around her desk and gestured for Angel to sit down. She looked around at the various diplomas and letters and pictures on the headteacher's office walls, realising that – thankfully – she'd never really had much reason to find herself in there.

'Don't worry,' the older brunette lady said, taking in Angel's expression. 'It's nothing serious. I just wanted a quiet spot to have a little word with you about next term. As you know, Angel, we have a system in place whereby we pick two new student heads of school each year – one for winter and one for spring and summer terms . . .'

'Yes?' Angel said, a little bit confused.

'Well, I've been wanting to save up this final head of school position for someone truly exceptional.'

'Right?'

Mrs Black broke into a wide smile. 'It's you, Angel. I want you to take the position for the second half of the year. I know you're going to make your classmates really proud. We faculty members were all in agreement. We see the incredible things you've done with the school fundraiser, and all the excellent work you're doing in class, and so we thought it was the perfect fit, if you're up for it?'

'Err . . . wow!' Angel said. 'Yes? I mean, yes! That's amazing. Thank you, miss!'

Mrs Black stood up, and Angel did, too. 'I thought that might give you a little boost before your exam for Dunstable Academy tomorrow. We're all really rooting for you, and I've already sent your transcript over to the head there with my recommendation, and this news. No young lady here would be worthier of a position at that school. Fingers crossed, eh?'

Angel wasn't sure what to say, so she just flapped her mouth open and shut like a goldfish for a few moments. Being the student head would probably look good on her application, but it would also give her a chance to really help some of the younger students in the school, maybe even give them the confidence to see they could do stuff too. She never would have thought when she had started at the school in Year Seven that by her final term she'd be student head! It made her feel more confident that other things might actually work out . . .

'OK, well, have a great lunch and a lovely Christmas if I don't spot you before the end of the day,' Mrs Black was saying. 'Though I might see you on the ice tonight!'

Angel just about managed to restrain herself from hugging her headteacher before she left the office and rushed to the canteen to give Izzy and Ola the frankly mind-blowing news. Maybe she

 311 ♥

would really be in with a chance at Dunstable Academy after all!

'Wow, Ange, you totally deserve this,' Izzy said, squeezing her tightly. Then she pulled back with a mock-serious face. 'But don't be thinking you can boss me and O around just because you're some fancy head girl now!'

Angel looked around the canteen to see if she could spot Caspar, but he was nowhere to be seen amongst his friends. She meant to go over and ask Josh if he was still ill, but by the time she had eaten lunch and soaked up more congratulations from her friends, it was time to go back to class. Most of English was taken up with Mr Henley's dramatic readings from *A Christmas Carol* while people passed notes and tried not to openly laugh, and then a final lesson of double history similarly descended into chaos. But still no sign of Caspar. As she headed to the room where the school council were gathering to get the supplies together to head over to the ice rink, she messaged him again. He replied:

I'm cool. Already over at the hospice. Got one final surprise . . .

Angel really wasn't sure how she felt about any more surprises today, but she set about making sure that everyone grabbed the collection buckets, decorations and other supplies they needed to set up for the final fundraiser at the ice rink, even as Tilda gave her a slight side-eye for directing everyone. Angel just didn't want them to miss anything. The group decided to walk over rather than jumping on the bus, and Sanj led them in some slightly less-than-tuneful renditions of Christmas carols as they went.

'OK, maybe we'll leave it to the choir when we get there,' he said jokingly.

Angel looked around the rink and over towards the hospice as they arrived, but there was still no sign of Caspar. She was feeling a mixture of anxiety and annoyance, but didn't really have time to think about it now. Instead, she and Olivia started stringing up the bluebells that Caspar had carefully packaged in a box, and they also put up a few more fairy lights and signs about the fundraiser. There were a couple of stalls set up by the local people from the fair, too, and as people slowly began to arrive, Sanj gathered the choir members together and they began to sing. It really was magical! Especially when Angel realised that as the evening began to draw in, there were little snowflakes beginning to drift down on to the ice!

'This is amazing!' She heard a familiar voice behind her and turned to see Ola and Izzy heading up behind her.

'Thanks, Ola!'

'Yeah, you might even get me out on that ice again, seeing as it's for a good cause and all,' Izzy added. Then she (for once) lowered her voice and added, 'Where's loverboy?'

Angel shrugged, picking up a collection bucket and sighing. 'Still no sign of him, but we need to head over and collect the patients from the hospice now. Do you guys want to come and help?'

Izzy and Ola agreed enthusiastically, and so

Angel corralled a small group of the student council members as a welcoming party to go and let the hospice know they were ready for them. They walked the short distance jingling their buckets, and Angel was thrilled to see so many people dropping coins in as they passed the group, headed towards the ice rink.

When they arrived at the hospice, Angel's mum came out to greet them, folding her arms in her scrubs against the drifting snow and chilly wind.

'Look at this!' she called, grinning.

'Are the patients all ready to go?' Angel enquired, a little surprised to see her. She glanced past her towards the hospice entrance. 'We've come to take them to the rink.'

'I know, but I've been told to stall you guys for a second. Someone has a little surprise for you . . . Well, he says it's for everyone, but I'm pretty sure it's mainly for you,' her mum said with a wink at her daughter.

Angel frowned, linking arms with her as they hurried into the warmth of the hospice lobby. But she stopped short as she saw the vision that greeted them when the group came through the sliding doors. Caspar was standing in front of the wall behind the admission desk – a wall that used to be pretty empty and a dull yellowish colour. But now, he pulled down a big white sheet to reveal a painted mural in beautiful blues and greens.

'Wow . . .' she breathed. The image was of lots of different patients, and the nurses and doctors that helped at the hospice, in abstract renderings that were unmistakeably Caspar's work. He began to walk over with a big smile on his face, as the people in the lobby clapped. The patients who were about to head to the rink were wheeled in, already dressed in warm clothes, coats, scarves and hats. Everyone congratulated Caspar, whooping and clapping him on the back. Angel even spotted her mum among the people he'd painted on the wall. She had planned to wait until there was a bit less of a crowd around him, but she was surprised to find him meeting her eyes as she hung back, and he made his way over to her.

'Hey ...' he said, scratching his eyebrow sheepishly. Angel had to swallow to remember how to speak, he looked so handsome!

'Hey yourself,' she said. 'So this is where you've been hiding. Just casually doing your very own Chagall mural?'

'Yeah, you know,' Caspar replied, dusting off his shoulder with a laugh. 'It was actually a lot of work but Rubes was out here when she could be, telling me when I'd got the proportions wrong and stuff.'

'Caspar, it's incredible,' Angel said, staring at the mural again, then turning back to him. 'This whole place feels more vibrant already. But ... speaking of that, where is Ruby?'

She saw Caspar's face grow a little bit more serious. 'She got a mild infection after one of her infusions this week, and they've said it's best if she rests.' Angel could see the concern on his face, and reached out to take his hand without thinking. Caspar looked down at their hands, then up at Angel in what looked like surprise. Angel drew in a deep breath, thinking that now seemed like a good time to talk about everything that had come to light in the last few days, but just as she was about to speak to Caspar about it, Tilda came over and Angel gently let go of his hand.

'Angel, shouldn't we be getting the patients out to the rink? That's, like, the whole point of your fundraiser tonight, no?' She waited, looking between Angel and Caspar, clearly oblivious to the fact that she was interrupting A Moment. Or maybe not so oblivious . . .

'You're right,' Angel said, sighing. She turned back to Caspar. 'We'd better get going,' she said apologetically.

'Cool, yeah definitely – I'll just finish up here and I'll be at the rink right after you.' He winked that signature wink and Angel tried not to melt into a puddle as he walked back over to his mural.

But then she heard Tilda call out, 'See you tomorrow if we don't catch up tonight, Cas. You'll pick me up at seven, right . . .?'

What? Angel froze. Was Caspar going to take Tilda to the disco? She'd completely messed up her chance with him, so of course he was. Mustering all her strength, Angel plastered a smile on to her face as she re-joined the group to head back out to the rink, feeling as cold as the ice they'd be skating on.

CHAPTER 24

By the time Angel, the other council members and the hospice helpers had escorted their star guests – the patients – over to the ice rink, things were in full swing, and snowflakes were steadily drifting down, too. The whole scene was magical, even if Angel was finding it hard to enjoy the atmosphere after what she'd heard back at the hospice. Still, the air was scented deliciously with spiced cider and mulled wine. The choir finished up some of their carols and then the skating rink's PA system fired up with Angel's personally curated playlist of Christmas hits (heavy on the Mariah Carey, of course). Angel couldn't help a small smile as she saw Josh and Sanj skating around the rink holding hands, but seeing them so happy reminded her all over again of how she'd missed her chance with Caspar. She would be firmly relegated to the friend zone now, surely.

They began to guide the patients in their wheelchairs out on to the ice, and Angel did feel a small surge of happiness at the delighted whoops that so many of them let out as their wheels glided along. It all felt worth the ups and downs they'd been through to get to that point. The stall with information about the hospice was buzzing with people talking to volunteers and collecting flyers, as well as making donations in the buckets. It totally felt like what the Christmas spirit was all about. She even saw Izzy hanging on to the back of a woman from the hospice's wheelchair, both of them laughing uproariously – Angel was pretty sure that it was because the chair was keeping Izzy from falling flat on her bum on the cold ice rather than the woman needing a push!

But she wasn't sure what to think when she saw Caspar strapping on his skates and gliding out on to the ice to meet her twenty minutes later. Wordlessly, to her total surprise, he took her hand and they began skating in a slow circle as the choir took up again with a soulfully slow number. Angel was, to say the very least, confused, but couldn't quite find the words to ask Caspar about Tilda and the Secret Santa stuff, so she stayed mute.

'Are you OK?' Caspar asked eventually. 'I know you might be a bit weirded out. I have it on good authority that the cat's out of the bag when it comes to the gifts you've been getting . . .'

'Yeah. I suppose my Secret Santa isn't so secret any more,' Angel said, turning to look at him and trying not to wobble on her skates as he was illuminated in the glow of the fairy lights dotted around them. He gripped her hand harder as she lost a step, which definitely didn't help her wobbles . . . 'B-but it's totally fine, I know it's just a friendship thing. I'm fine with that.'

'Oh.'

Angel came to a shaky halt by gripping on to the side wall of the rink, and Caspar glided to a stop beside her. 'Yeah, I mean, I know you're seeing Tilda and stuff—'

'Whoa, whoa, whoa. Angel, I'm not seeing Tilda.'

'But I heard her mention about you taking her to the disco tomorrow, and—'

She stopped, because Caspar was grinning and shaking his head. 'Not if I can go with who I really want to go with,' he said. 'It was a group thing anyway. I know I've been tip-toeing around things a bit with you, Angel. I was just scared to come out and say . . . Well, lots of things, but when you didn't seem to be getting the hint the other day in the art room, I guess—'

It was Angel's turn to shake her head. 'No! I mean . . . NO!' She hadn't meant to sound even more emphatic, but that was how it came out. 'I'm just not very good at any of this stuff.'

Caspar edged a bit closer. 'What kind of stuff is that, AG?' His eyes bored into her, and he took her hand again.

Angel began to sweat, and mumbled, 'I don't know.'

Caspar straightened up a bit, still holding on to her gloved hand. 'Well, *I* do. I want you to come with me to the disco tomorrow night. I mean, I know you've got the exam tomorrow, but you might want something to take your mind off it all afterwards, right? I'd love to go with you. Specifically you, regardless of who else might be in the group.' He smiled, his eyes crinkling adorably.

Angel pretended for about a millisecond that she had to think it over, but then nodded enthusiastically. 'Definitely. I'd . . . I'd really like that. Thanks, Caspar!' Just as she spoke, the choir finished their last round of songs, and the rink manager announced that the fundraiser skate was coming to an end before they opened up the rink to the wider public again.

Caspar and Angel went over to where the rest of the council were gathering with their collection buckets. After a quick look inside each of them, Angel was certain they must have made over five hundred pounds! Together with what they'd raised with the film screenings, they'd surely be close to £750 in total for the hospice.

'This is amazing. Thanks soooo much everyone,' she said, as they all high-fived and cheered at what they'd achieved. It had been a bit bumpy, but Angel knew this was definitely close to one of her best days ever. She couldn't wait to tell her mum about how much they'd raised!

She went over to give Izzy and Ola a hug goodbye and thank them for all their support, and saw Caspar laughing and joking with his friends too. At the back of her mind was still the fact that even if today *was* one of her best days, tomorrow would be one of the most important for her future. And not just because of her first official date with Caspar – or ever!

'You've got that "I need to study" look on your mug again, Ange,' Izzy said, elbowing her gently in the ribs. 'As well as the smitten kitten one.'

'I am kind of thinking I need to get home and cram some last-minute revision in,' Angel confessed. She hugged Izzy and Ola again, and then gave Caspar a quick text goodbye so that she could make a relatively swift get-away without all his friends making her blush. As she walked home, though, she almost floated off the pavement when she read his reply:

You are going to ace it tomorrow, I know it. You're the smartest girl I know. Love, Secret Caspar ;) x

She knew it was just a play on the sign-offs on his Secret Santa cards, but the whole idea made it almost – almost! – too hard for Angel to concentrate on her cramming. But as she got her books out, knowing Caspar believed in her made her all the more determined. She almost couldn't wait to finally sit the Dunstable Academy exam!

CHAPTER 25

Saturday 20th December

'When was the last time you drove?' Angel asked her mother dubiously as they approached the kerbside and she saw the red Vauxhall sitting there.

'I was driving before you were born, my girl!' Ruth said, slotting the key into the door and opening the car with a grin over the roof.

'Exactly . . .' Angel muttered.

'Come on, hop in!'

Angel had to admit, it was really nice of Victor to lend her mum his car for the day so that Ruth could drive Angel over to Dunstable Academy for the exam. But as she settled into the seat beside her mum, she wasn't sure she fully trusted that it was an entirely good idea. Still, her advent calendar had challenged her to **Let go and trust!** this morning, so she decided to focus on the task at hand. With her mum cheerfully singing along to the radio as they drove, Angel managed to ignore the nerves churning in her stomach from both Ruth's driving abilities and the exam. That is, until they pulled up and she saw the other students all arriving too. There were only five places up for grabs for the scholarship, and this was her competition.

Her mum cut off the engine, but made no move just yet to get out. Angel stopped reaching for the door handle when she saw Ruth's expression.

'Angel, I want you to know, again, how proud I am of you. And how much I wish you wouldn't *need* a scholarship to afford to go here,' her mum said, gesturing towards the red-brick building in front of them. 'But no matter what happens, you're an absolute star, and you will be an incredible success. All right?'

Her mum clearly knew it was best not to give too much time to ponder her motivational words, so she just reached over and squeezed Angel's hand, before opening the car door and getting out. Angel followed suit, and together they strode with their heads held high towards the block where the exam was going to be held.

As Angel sat down at the small desk and arranged her pencil case, she felt her palms sweating and her throat going dry.

'Begin,' the examiner said in a stark voice, and Angel swallowed as she opened up the booklet. But as she got into it, she felt more and more at ease as her answers flowed. She didn't want to get over-confident about it, but she had a feeling she'd done pretty well by the time the exam concluded. More than anything, she felt a huge weight lift off her shoulders. After all, there wasn't much more she could do about it now but wait and see whether she got offered a place and a scholarship – and that news wouldn't come until the beginning of January.

Afterwards, Angel walked towards the car where her mum was waiting on a cushion of airy relief. But she could tell that something was wrong when she got to her mum's door and saw her on the phone. Through the slightly open window she could hear Ruth saying, 'Ah, Angel's finished now. I'll be there in a bit, Evan. OK.'

Angel frowned, her high from finishing the exam slightly dampened even as her mum opened the car door to jump out and give her a hug.

'How did it go, darling?' she asked eagerly.

'I think really well,' Angel said, still a bit cautious. 'At least it's all done now, anyway!'

'I bet you've done amazingly, sweetheart.'

Angel took a step back. 'What's up, Mum?'

Ruth avoided her eyes. 'Well . . . I might have to go in to work this afternoon. We're a bit short staffed and . . . I can't really tell you more about it, darling, you know about the patient confidentiality. Maybe check in with Caspar, eh?'

Angel and her mum got back into the car, and Angel could already see a missed call and a voicemail message on her phone from Caspar as she switched it back on.

'*Hey Angel . . .*' She couldn't help the tingles that spread down her spine just at hearing his voice. '*Really hope the exam went well! Can you give me a call back whenever you get a sec? It's about tonight.*'

Angel's heart sank, but he sounded so dejected about it himself that she knew it must be something pretty serious. It wasn't ideal to have to speak to him in the close confines of the car with her mum, but she couldn't hold off finding out what Caspar wanted to talk about until they got home. So, reluctantly, Angel hit dial on Caspar's number.

'Angel? Hey!' She smiled at how quickly he'd answered the phone.

'Hey.'

'How did it go? Left those other students trembling from the flames coming from your exam paper, right?'

Angel brushed her shoulders off even though he couldn't see it, and chuckled. 'I dunno about that, but I think it went really well. Guess I'll just have to wait and see now, though.'

'I'll have the air horns ready to celebrate the moment you hear about it,' he said, his deep voice making Angel flush. She turned away from her mum and her silently too-pleased smile as she steered the car around a roundabout. 'Listen, I've got kind of bad news about tonight. I know this is really rubbish timing, but Rubes needs to go to St Ted's for a proper hospital stay overnight tonight.'

'Oh no, is everything OK?' Angel's brows knitted in concern, and she glanced over at her mum again now, but Ruth's smile was a bit more reassuring now.

'Yeah, it's nothing too serious, but she needs to get a new port fitted, and my mum's away on a business trip and Rubes gets quite nervous about stuff like that, so I thought it might be better if I went with her and my dad over there tonight.'

'Yeah, of course!' Angel said sincerely. The thought of going into a hospital was scary enough as a teenager, and even though Ruby went to the hospice a lot, Angel understood how this would feel different. 'Don't worry about it at all, Caspar. We'll have plenty of other chances to . . . um . . . go on . . .'

'Our first date?' he finished, his voice soft. Angel blushed from head to toe, fully regretting calling him while they were still in the car.

'Err, yeah,' she replied, cringing at her mum's still-silent but louder-than-loud grin as she stared through the windscreen. Thankfully they were turning on to their street at last.

'Well, please make sure you let your hair down tonight. I'm definitely regretting not being able to have a dance and see those braids swinging,' Caspar said, just as Angel's mum cut the engine. She hoped beyond hope that the sound didn't carry through the phone.

'Mmhmmm,' Angel said, biting her lip. 'I'll do my best. Izz and Ola will get me on the dance floor no doubt!'

'Have an amazing time . . . and erm, keep tomorrow free? I'm hoping I can make this up to you,' he added, sounding very much like he was planning something but trying to sound casual.

'OK . . .' Angel said, suspiciously, as she got out of the car and followed her mum into the house.

'See you soon, Angel Green,' Caspar said. She could practically hear him winking.

'Bye,' she replied. Her mum still had that over-pleased look on her face as Angel hung up the phone. 'Say nada, Mum,' she warned through a smile.

Ruth held up her hands. 'I'm saying nothing.'

'Uh huh.'

But she felt just as giddy as if Caspar was actually taking her to the disco tonight. What did he have planned for tomorrow?

CHAPTER 26

'It's a good thing you're well on the path to becoming a doctor, Ange, because I am, like, completely on the verge of a heart attack. You guys have to come here. Stat! I've already told Ola. She's ten minutes out.'

Angel laughed. Izzy had clearly been watching too many medical dramas again. 'It's five o'clock, Izz,' Angel said down the phone. 'The disco doesn't even start until half seven, and we definitely don't want to be the first to arrive.'

'Exactly. I've got T-minus three hours or so to get this whole look together. It's like a hurricane

has been through my wardrobe. I need assistance!'
Angel waited. 'Plus I'll let you borrow my green
dress.'

Angel nodded even though Izzy couldn't see
her, of course. 'OK, sold. See you in a bit!'

She smiled as she hung up the phone, knowing
full well that she would have gone round to Izzy's
house to get ready anyway. She got her things
together, only a little bit sad that Caspar wouldn't
be at the disco that evening. She was still looking
forward to celebrating the fact that she'd got the
exam behind her at last, and witnessing the
excitement of Izzy's semi-date with Manny, too.

She arrived at Izzy's house, but it was Ola who
answered the door, with a haunted look in her
eyes. 'Thank goodness you're here. She's driving
me up the wall already.' Both Angel and Ola
laughed, but with a hint of caution given how
much Izzy could get herself into a tizzy over things
like this.

Ola filled Angel in on the fact that Izzy's dad,
sister and stepmum were away for the night, which

was perhaps both a good and a bad thing. Angel thought that Izzy's assessment of her room looking like a hurricane had passed through it was probably being generous. It seemed like every single item in her wardrobe was now strewn across her bed and floor.

'I have *nothing* to wear!' Izzy declared as soon as Angel walked in.

Ola held Angel's gaze. 'See what we're dealing with?'

But an hour of talking their friend round to her very first dress choice, then starting in on her shoes, and then another thirty minutes of sorting out their own outfits and doing each other's makeup, and Angel, Izzy and Ola were finally ready. Angel had opted for her favourite trainers to go with Izzy's fun green dress, which really worked against her skin tone, and Izzy's body-con blue number was making her seem extra confident, too. Angel knew *that* was what would really make Manny take notice. And Ola looked lovely too, her yellow maxi dress comfortable but dramatic – perfect for her!

'We look *fit*!' Izzy declared, initiating a sequence of selfies. Twenty pictures later, with numerous different poses, they found a couple they were all happy with. But at last, they were headed to the school for the disco. They were meeting up with some of their classmates there, but the most important thing – mainly to Izzy – was that Manny had messaged to say he would meet her at the gates.

'There they are!' Izzy said as they approached the school, with their winter coats and scarves over their dresses. Manny, Sanj and Josh were hovering by the gates, and waved as they saw the girls approach. 'Oh my gosh, look how good Manny looks. What if I can't do this?'

'You can, and you will,' Angel said, squeezing her friend's gloved hand. 'Let's have some fun!'

They made their way over to the boys, and Angel felt a swell of warmth again as she saw how into each other Sanj and Josh were. But most of all, she and Ola let out silent squeals as they linked arms in front of Izzy and Manny, who offered their friend a crooked elbow as they all headed towards the cloakroom to dump their coats.

'Wow, this is surreal!' Angel heard Manny exclaim, looking around the school. 'I haven't been back here for two years.' He glanced down at Izzy. 'But you'll be over at the college soon, right? Only a term and your exams left. That'll be cool . . .'

This might actually turn into a thing! Angel thought happily, watching her friend giggle and chat to Manny.

They all got some punch, and admired how Tilda and the other students on the committee had actually put together a convincingly frosty and fantasy-medieval theme to the décor. The DJ was playing all the best tunes, and Angel and her friends were soon shaking everything they had on the dance floor. Watching Sanj and Josh, and Izzy and Manny pairing off did make Angel a little jealous. But she sent Caspar a few pics of them all dancing, and he messaged back to say how happy he was that Angel was having a good time – and a really sweet picture of him and Ruby in her hospital room with their dad.

She's doing well. Go check your locker. Secret Santa might have left you one last present . . . x

'Enough with the phone!' Ola said, shimmying towards Angel, but when she showed her friend Caspar's message, she gave Angel a sly grin. 'Oh, let's go.'

'I'm not sure we're really meant to be sneaking around the rest of the school, though,' Angel said, looking around the assembly hall dubiously. Mrs Black was deep in conversation with one of the other teachers, and there were other chaperones but nobody near the door that lead to the corridors.

'Come on!' Ola said, so Angel took a deep breath and grabbed her outstretched hand. They tried to look casual as they sidled up to the door and slipped out. The corridors weren't dark like Angel had expected, and there were a handful of students mingling around them, with a bored-looking chaperone dad posted on the other side of the door back into the disco.

'OK, less dramatic than I anticipated,' Ola said, sounding disappointed. But they made their way to Angel's locker and she opened it and peered inside. A little box wrapped in the familiar paper that all her other Secret Santa gifts had come in was nestled inside it, with a note attached.

One last surprise. Tomorrow, 10am at the coach station . . .
Love, Cas/Secret Santa x

Angel grinned at the message, even as intrigue swarmed her brain. What could it be?

'Open it!' Ola encouraged.

Angel tore open the package to reveal a little wooden model.

'Did he make that?' her friend asked, and Angel turned it around in her hands, nodding – she was certain he had. It was a little abstract version of lots of famous London sights.

'Whoa . . . I think . . . I think we might be going

to London tomorrow!' Angel whispered, then looked up at Ola with a grin that now almost hurt.

'Niiiice!' Ola exclaimed, swinging Angel around in the hallway. 'OK, we'd better get back to the dancing. Though I suppose you need to start conserving your energy for your trip to the Big Smoke tomorrow. Gah, how romantic! Between you and Izzy I'm going to get a toothache with all this sweet stuff going on for you guys!'

They started walking back to the hall. 'You don't have to worry that we'll splinter off with these boys though, Ola ...' Angel began cautiously, suddenly concerned that might be what her friend was thinking. But Ola nudged her gently with her shoulder.

'I know, babe. If this stuff has taught me anything, it's that when you're ready for it, romance will find you. For now, I'm going to use this all as inspo for my new dramatic project. I might write a romantic comedy or something, who knows!'

They finished up the night back on the dance floor, with Angel giddy about what Caspar had in store for the next day ...

CHAPTER 27

Sunday 21st December

Angel wasn't quite sure if her feet were actually touching the carpet as she headed downstairs *waaay* too early the next morning. She was nervous, that was for sure, but she was also so excited she could hardly contain herself. That was, until she came over to the kitchen table and saw the post. Her mum must have been looking at the letters when she got home late last night. Angel had crashed out after the disco. Usually her mum put the bills and stuff away, but they were still out, so maybe she'd been too tired and forgotten. Angel could see that there was an awful lot of red on the pages, and a worrying number of 'OVERDUE' notices. Were things really that bad? And, Angel thought, her mum always went all out for Christmas, knowing that it was the time of year when missing her dad really came to the very forefront of Angel's mind. She was probably worried about buying presents, too.

Feeling sobered, Angel quickly made her mum a cup of tea, then grabbed the bills and took it all up to Ruth's room. She knocked gently then edged the door open, but she was surprised to see her mum sitting up in bed, headscarf still tied around her head and her glasses perched on her nose as she typed out a text with a smile. It widened as she saw Angel enter, and Ruth feigned clutching her heart.

'Wow. It's a good thing you're going to be training as a doctor, sweetheart, because I think I'm about to have a heart attack,' she said good-naturedly, eyes on the cup of tea that Angel set down on the bedside table. 'To what do I owe the pleasure?'

Angel's smile was half-hearted as she held up the bills in her other hand. 'I was going to ask about these,' she said softly. 'I know things have been tough . . . I was thinking, and I should have thought about this before, but I've been too caught-up in studying for that exam, but maybe over the break I can start looking for some part-time work and—'

But to Angel's surprise, her mum was still smiling, and patted her duvet, gesturing for Angel to sit down.

'No, no, no, darling. Thank you so much for offering, and I know this looks worrying. For a time there, it was. But you're not going to believe this. A genuine Christmas miracle has occurred!'

Angel studied her mum's face dubiously. 'Lottery win?'

'OK, maybe not that miraculous. But . . . I've got a promotion at the hospice! Head of nursing!'

Angel jumped up, and her mum kicked her legs excitedly under the covers like a little kid. Swiftly, Angel sat back down again. 'Mum. Oh my gosh!

That's amazing. You soooo deserve it!' She grabbed her mum and gave her a massive hug, then pulled back to look into her eyes. 'Mum . . . You're really my biggest inspiration. I would never be doing all this medical stuff if it wasn't for you!'

Her mum grinned even as she blinked back tears, which Angel felt prickling in her eyes too.

'That's so amazing to hear, darling. But, most of all? Goodbye, red bills! Hello, boiler insurance! Heck, maybe even a car of our own?'

Angel thought back to her mum's dubious skills on the road yesterday morning. 'Hmm, one step at a time, eh?' She glanced at her mum's phone as it rested on the bedside table. 'I guess you've told Victor the good news?' she asked, and her mum nodded.

'He's really proud of me, too.'

Angel took a deep breath. 'Errm . . . So what's he up to over the Christmas break? Maybe we could all get together?'

Her mum looked so pleased she might burst. 'That would be lovely, Angel! He'll be so pleased.

I'll keep the big day for just the two of us, like always, but maybe Boxing Day . . .'

'Sounds good!' Angel noticed the time on the alarm clock by her mum's bed. 'Oh wow, I'd better get going,' she said, feeling giddy again.

'Of course, the big day!' her mum said. Angel frowned.

'Hang on a sec . . . I haven't had a chance to tell you about Caspar's invitation yet! How do *you*—'

Her mum tapped her nose, but then immediately confessed. 'He's a very smart and polite young man, and he asked me for permission, of course. Otherwise, there would be no way you'd be gallivanting off to London without my knowledge. In fact, when were you planning to ask, eh?'

'What do you think the cuppa was for?' Angel asked with a chuckle.

'Go, go, go, darling. Have a wonderful time. Check in with me, and be safe. But most of all, the first one.' She reached over to hug Angel once more, and peck her cheek.

'I will. See you this evening!' Angel called, hurrying

out of the door to check her outfit, makeup, braids and everything else one more time before heading to the bus station to meet the boy of her dreams!

10:06. Angel stared at the time on her phone's screen atop the smiling picture of her and her mum. Was she being stood up? She knew that time-keeping wasn't exactly Caspar Johnson's strong suit, but this was getting ridiculous. The bright winter sunshine made everything seem cheery as she waited on the corner at the entrance to the coach station, watching people bustling in carrying bags of presents, heading home for the holidays. But in a way, Angel couldn't help thinking it was inevitable that this would all fall apart at the last moment – she didn't *want* to be negative, but things that seemed too good to be true often were . . .

She heard footsteps pounding up behind her and whipped around, squinting as she turned into the direction of the sunlight.

'Angel!' Caspar called, speeding towards her and waving. In no time, given his athleticism, he was skidding to a halt in front of her, panting lightly and grinning widely. 'OK for once it's not my fault I'm late – the bus was. But I'm here, we're here . . . you're here.' He slowed down and looked at Angel as though he was finally able to take things in. He reached over and ran his fingertips along one of her braids as they hung down from her woolly hat. 'Hey.'

'Hey yourself,' Angel managed, the shakiness of her voice giving away just how much he was forgiven for his lateness.

'OK, come on – the coach leaves in five!' Grabbing her hand, Caspar wove them in between the families with small children trying to wrestle themselves on to the coach, and whipped out his phone to show the ticket inspector. She scanned the codes on his screen with a smile, then turned away to shout, 'The 10:15 to London will depart shortly. Any more passengers, this way please!'

Still gripping on to Angel's hand – she was very glad she wasn't wearing gloves at the moment – Caspar checked their seat numbers, then gestured for her to take the window seat. 'You should get to see all the sights,' he said, 'as long as you don't mind me leaning over your shoulder.' He quirked a smile her way, and she tried not to flush.

'I'll tolerate it,' she quipped, settling into the coach seat. She felt a thrill of excitement zip through her as the coach began to pull out of the station. She was actually on her way to London – and with Caspar Johnson. This was definitely a Christmas for the books!

'Caspar,' she said, turning to find him closer than she anticipated. 'I just wanted to say thank you so much for this. Nobody's ever done anything like this for me . . .' She looked down at her lap, embarrassed, but he reached for her hand as it lay on the armrest, and took it in his again. She turned to meet his eyes. 'And all the Secret Santa gifts, too. Especially the calendar! It's really helped me out a lot these past few weeks!'

He chuckled. 'Yeah, the calendar was something I started out doing with Ruby, just funny little sayings and stuff, but I started playing around with them and thought I'd make one that was a bit more motivational, I suppose!'

'It worked!'

'You deserve all of it, Angel Green,' he told her, then smiled. 'Besides, turns out I got a fair bit out of it too.' He looked down at their intertwined hands. 'You'll see – we've got some fun stuff in store. But mainly, I get you all to myself.' He lifted their hands, and placed a light kiss on the back of her hand that made her completely and utterly melt. She turned away so he wouldn't see how much it affected her.

They watched the rolling green fields on the sides of the motorway turn into more houses and taller buildings as they finally began to approach the city. Angel felt the anticipation building inside her to breaking point, but Caspar just looked happy and more than a little bit smug as she turned to check his reaction when they pulled in to Victoria coach station.

Everything felt buzzy and vivid and exciting as Caspar led her off the coach, and they moved through the bustle of the area and towards the tube station.

'Pleaaase tell me where we're going,' Angel said as they touched their bank cards against the yellow card readers to move through the barriers. Caspar shook his head, miming a zip over his mouth . . . which made Angel look at his lips . . . which made her ignore the sign that she should stand on the right of the escalator. Caspar put an arm around her and moved her to stand on the step in front of him as they sailed down into the belly of the station. Angel tried to ignore the warmth of his body behind her, and the way one hand rested on her shoulder as they descended. She stepped off the escalator clumsily, and then both she and Caspar were distracted by an incredible busker in the area that led to the tube train platforms. As the girl sang and played her acoustic guitar in a soulful rendition of a song Angel knew was called *This Christmas* – originally by Donny Hathaway, one of her mum's all-time favourites – Caspar pulled Angel next to the girl's marked-out busking 'stage', put one hand on Angel's waist and the other gripping her free hand, and led her in a slow dance. She looked up into his big, hazel eyes and felt both completely out of her comfort zone and perfectly comfortable at the same time. Without speaking, she instinctively stepped in closer to Caspar as they swayed, and rested her head on his shoulder for a moment.

'OK maybe I'm not in such a hurry to get wherever it is you're taking me,' she said, just as the girl – looking almost apologetically over at Angel – finished the song. She and Caspar broke apart and both gave her a round of applause. Caspar dropped a few coins into the girls upturned hat, and she nodded at both of them in thanks as she struck up her next song. A few moments later, they were crushed on to a tube train, heading to their mystery destination.

'It's Sunday! Where are all these people going?' Angel asked, used to the calm of their home town.

Caspar chuckled. 'All right, out-of-towner!

They're probably all sorting out their last-minute Christmas presents!'

Angel glanced at him guiltily. 'Actually, I need to do a bit of that if we can, since you mentioned it!'

He rolled his eyes, stealing her usual expression. 'You're lucky I like you, AG, because I have to say, shopping is not up there with my favourite pastimes . . .'

'Oh, so all your pressies are sorted, are they?' she asked, raising an eyebrow. They were jostled closer together by a Spanish family looking eagerly at their guidebooks.

'Well,' Caspar said quietly, 'I'm sorting out the most important one right now.' Before she could respond, he told her that this was their stop, and led her out of the train's sliding doors at a station that Angel realised was Embankment. He guided her out of the station and on to the Strand. Angel remembered reading that the famous Savoy hotel was on this busy road, but she doubted that Caspar's budget stretched to that.

'Tell me where we're going!' she said through a laugh, tugging on the hand that Caspar had stretched out to get her to keep up with his long strides.

'Patience, AG. We're almost there!'

Suddenly he paused at an opening in the buildings, and she stared as she saw a beautiful courtyard, bordered on each side by a magnificent Georgian building. It was illuminated by stunning uplights in the fading winter sunlight. But most importantly, right in the centre of the courtyard was a *huge* ice rink!

'Wow!' she breathed.

Caspar looked over at her with a grin. 'I thought since we never got to have a dance together at the disco, this would be the perfect opportunity to take you somewhere really special. Somerset House does this every year. Pretty amazing, isn't it?'

'Uh, yeah!' Angel replied, wandering further in as the music playing around the skating rink swelled. The ice was busy with skaters, but Caspar pointed to a sign that said there would be a professional display in an hour's time.

'I took the liberty of requesting your mum steal these from your room, and she handed them over when I saw her at the hospice,' he said, suddenly pulling a familiar pair of fluffy yellow socks out of his pocket. 'I hope they're clean, because they've been in here for a while!'

Angel pulled a face through her smile, and yanked them out of his hands. 'Thanks, *Santa*,' she said. 'Come on, let's hire some skates!'

Caspar nodded, but said, 'This is all on me, though. *I'll* be hiring them, since this is our first date and I invited you. If you're lucky I might even buy you a hot chocolate,' he said with that gorgeously infuriating wink. 'Next date is on you, though.'

She nudged him with her elbow, but he just stretched an arm around her shoulders and guided her towards the skate hire booth. A few moments later, they were teasing each other as they laced up their skates, their necks craning to watch the skaters already on the ice. Even with the increasing cold, Angel felt warm and light and excited.

Caspar took her hand, and they made their way out on to the rink. It was like their local one, but even better! Everything was big and bold and crowded and bright. Angel loved it! There were skaters of all abilities, some whizzing around the centre of the ice in perfect swirls, others clinging anxiously to the sides, reminding Angel fondly of Izzy. She'd not had a chance to respond to her friends' good luck messages this morning, but for now she was happy just being in Caspar's company.

He was watching her with a gaze that made Angel feel really *seen* as he held her hand while they looped around the ice, his strides strong and confident. Even when a couple of girls who were around their age skated past, giggling and making it pretty obvious that they were checking Caspar out, he seemed to only have eyes for her. Angel could feel that tiny voice of doubt inside her that made her wonder if all this was going to come crashing down around her, if a boy like Caspar could really like a girl like her. But just as it tried to pipe up, he said, simply: 'I'm crazily happy right now, Angel Green.' And he squeezed her hand.

After a few more (butterfly-in-the-stomach) spins around the huge rink, an announcement came over the PA system that the rink needed to be cleared for a fifteen-minute professional display. Angel skated towards the exit with Caspar on her heels, and they rushed, laughing at one another as they struggled on to the rubber matting to get the best view of the ice. They managed to get right up against the barrier, in front of the few rows of staggered seating behind it, and watched eagerly as three couples skated out on to the ice in matching grey and blue outfits. A jazzy rendition of a familiar Christmas song began to pound out of the speakers, and Angel watched in awe as the skaters danced, flipped and twirled on the ice in time. And she'd thought *Caspar* was a good ice skater!

But Angel was distracted a little from the amazing display in front of them as two things happened. From the growing slate-grey sky above them, shot through with slashes of wintery sunlight, came a few fat flakes of snow. As Angel looked up to the sky, more began to fall, creating a wintery wonderland of drifting snow over the ice rink.

'Wow,' she breathed, then turned to Caspar. 'Did you plan this, too?'

But instead of joking back, she found him staring at her again.

'What?' she whispered. The snow was falling a little harder now but Angel hardly noticed. She finally looked away from the dreamy brown depths of Caspar's eyes as she noticed he was pulling off a glove. Then she felt his warm fingertips against her cheek, melting away a snowflake. Another fell on her eyelash and he leaned closer, a mysterious smile on his face. She blinked as he reached up gently to brush that one away too. Then she felt the cold of a flake on her lip. This time, he didn't use a fingertip. Instead, as Angel held her breath, she saw Caspar leaning his face down even closer to hers. He licked his own lips, and instinctively, her eyes drifted shut.

And then the most perfect part of the perfect

day: Caspar Johnson's lips pressed lightly, then more confidently, to hers.

They were warm and strong and delicious. Angel fought not to let her nerves overtake her as Caspar gently gripped her waist and moved his lips with a perfect pressure against hers. After what felt like forever, he finally pulled back, his eyes still closed even as Angel's opened.

'Now *that*,' he said, 'was wow.'

After basking in the moment a bit longer, Caspar offered to go and get them those hot chocolates he'd promised. The snow was coming down a little harder now, and Angel decided they should probably go inside for a bit – she had spotted a sign that meant she might be able to give Caspar a gift too. She grabbed her phone and made a few quick taps. As he returned with the delicious chocolatey drinks – even remembering her five marshmallows – she gave him a sly smile.

'So, obviously we'll be hitting the shops before we get the coach back home,' she began, raising an amused eyebrow at Caspar's faux-crestfallen reaction. 'But,' she continued, 'while we wait for the snow to settle a bit, there's something I think we should check out.'

Caspar sipped his drink, his expression puzzled. 'This is supposed to be *my* day of surprises, AG,' he said, but Angel gripped her warm drink in one hand and grabbed Caspar's with the other, leading him into the building. It was quite dauntingly grand and busy, but Angel spotted the signs for where she wanted to take Caspar, and eagerly led the way. Finally they stood in front of a large sign.

'Marc . . . Chagall?' Caspar read reverentially, looking at the large poster at the entrance to the exhibition. 'What? I had no idea they had an exhibition on here. I suppose I was too caught up with sorting out the ice skating!' he said. 'Oh, but you need tickets . . .'

Angel held up her phone. 'Lucky I've got some then, eh?'

Caspar grinned at her, but she strode away towards the attendant, who welcomed them in with a friendly smile as she scanned Angel's e-tickets.

They made their way into the more hushed environs of the exhibition, with Caspar gazing up rapturously at each of the paintings and tapestries. Even though they didn't have the tapestry that inspired his mural at the hospice, Angel had to admit that all of the works were beautiful.

'This is incredible, Angel. Thanks so much for getting the tickets.' He took her hand as they stood in front of a blue and white painting of a couple kissing. *Blue Lovers, 1914* read the description. Still looking at the painting, Caspar said, 'I just want to tell you, Angel – I've fancied you for a really long time. I'm glad I finally got the guts to tell you.'

Angel turned to him. 'I'm really glad, too.'

Then, mimicking the picture before them, Angel reached up and gently placed a hand on Caspar's cheek to turn him towards her. Smiling, she stood up on her tiptoes and brushed her lips against his. He pressed in closer, wrapping his arms around Angel's waist and lifting her until she felt like she was floating.

'Merry Christmas,' he whispered.

Saturday 10th January

Angel gripped the letter tighter in her hand as she strode through the cold Saturday morning air towards the hospice. She couldn't open this alone. She had to have her mum there, and she'd told Angel that she was going to Victor's for dinner that evening, so this was her only chance to catch her. Angel had just about come to terms with the idea of Victor – he'd come round on Boxing Day with mince pies that he'd made himself, and they'd genuinely had loads of fun playing the new dancing game on the games console Angel had got from her mum (even though Angel said it was too generous). She'd even remembered to get Victor a present through the giddy haze of being in London with Caspar for their epic first date before Christmas, and her mum's new man had seemed to like the flat cap Angel had got him.

Angel smiled soppily as she thought about Caspar. They'd spent loads of time together over the Christmas holidays, prompting Izzy to tell her in no uncertain terms that she a) had to be the maid of honour at her wedding to Caspar and b) that under no circumstances would they be stopping their traditional walks to school because of any boy. With great affection, Angel had told her that a) she needed to calm down and b) she needed to calm down! But she still couldn't quite believe she had a boyfriend!

But even though she did, there was nobody else she could imagine sharing this moment with – good or bad – than her mother. She turned down the pathway leading to the familiar sliding doors of the hospital, but just as they slid open, she saw another familiar sight. One that made her break into a goofy grin.

'AG!' a deep voice greeted her. 'What are you doing here?'

Caspar was in front of her in a few easy strides, kissing her lips softly. She blushed as she noticed his parents and Ruby behind him. 'I could ask the same thing of you? I assumed you'd be sleeping off your movie marathon with Josh last night.' They'd both agreed to hang out with their besties after school on Fridays.

'I can get my IVs at home!' Ruby chimed in from behind them, wheeling over and tugging at Angel's duffel coat. Angel bent down and gave Ruby a hug of greeting, waving to the Johnsons.

'Wow, really?' Angel said, glancing up at Caspar for confirmation.

He nodded. 'It's true. We're all learning how to give Rubes the infusions at home – the docs think it should be OK sometimes. So she won't have to come in here as much,' he said, ruffling the top of his sister's curls. She giggled, batting his hand away.

'Hey, Angel you're going to be a doctor so you should learn too!' Ruby said, grabbing Angel's hand as Nurse Evan gestured for the family to follow him into one of the treatment rooms.

Angel smiled. 'Maybe . . . there's something I need to do first though,' she said, and showed Caspar the unopened envelope, tapping at the stamp on the front of it.

'Dunstable . . . Wait, is that . . . ?'

Angel exhaled hard. 'That's what I'm going to find out. I need to open it with my mum.'

'Come and find me the moment you've done that, OK? I'll be just in here,' Caspar said, kissing Angel on the temple. She'd taken her braids out for now, and she loved the feel of his lips against the dense curls of her long afro.

'I will,' she said.

She found her mum behind the reception desk, briefing a couple of the other nurses. It was so cool to see her in her new role!

'Mum!' Angel called.

'Hey, darling. What's up?' her mum said, coming out from behind the desk to give Angel a hug. She pulled back, examining her daughter's face. Angel handed her the envelope.

'I need you to open it,' she said.

Her mum studied the envelope for a moment, then glanced up at Angel before tearing it open. But she paused before pulling the letter out, and said, 'I'm what?'

'Proud of me no matter what happens,' Angel repeated, staring at the piece of paper in her mum's hand that could determine her future. Ruth unfolded the page and scanned it, her face unreadable.

'Well?' Angel asked urgently.

'Well . . .' her mum began, and Angel's heart sank – but then it soared as her mum turned on her biggest, brightest grin. 'My daughter's a genius. You're in, Angel! *Full scholarship!*'

They both screamed, jumping up and down in the middle of the hospice foyer, until her mum stopped, realising people were staring.

'I'm SO happy for you, Angel. I knew you could do it!'

Angel squeezed her mum into a tight hug. 'Not without you, Mum,' she said. There was one other person she needed to tell. She jogged down the hallway and knocked tentatively at the door where Caspar's family were. When someone called to come in, she opened the door and all the Johnsons turned to her.

'Ow!' Ruby said, but was still grinning up at Angel as her mum practised inserting the IV under the nurse's supervision. 'Well?' the little girl asked. 'Cas told us you've got really important stuff in your letter. What did it say?'

Caspar stood up and moved towards Angel, studying her face. 'You got in,' he said quietly. How could he always read her like that? She thought she'd been doing a good job of hiding her excitement, but that was hard to do around Caspar Johnson.

'I got in,' she said. 'I got in!'

Caspar spun her around, whooping, and the rest of his family shouted their congratulations.

'Come on then, soon-to-be Doctor Green,' Caspar said, taking her hand and leading her towards his sister. 'You've got a lot to learn here. Next IV practice is yours!'

Angel laughed and pulled on the latex gloves. She realised suddenly that she'd found the boy of her dreams, she'd worked hard and she was on her way to where she really wanted to be. She was well and truly happy. This new year was going to be amazing!

The End

Here's a sneak peek at another heartwarming story you won't want to miss!

Chapter One

Tabitha Brown's heart thudded in her chest as she read the Instagram caption on her phone. *Best night with my favourite girls!*

She didn't want to look, but she couldn't help but scrutinise every inch of the picture – Jess, her blonde, crinkled hair flowing down her shoulders, with her arms round two other girls, all three beaming into the lens. They looked like the *best* of friends.

You really shouldn't be looking, Tabby thought. *There's absolutely no reason to.*

But still she did.

She was sprawled out on the lawn in her gran's back garden, a book open by her side – *Solitaire* by Alice Oseman – and prescription sunglasses over her face.

Gran's garden wasn't huge, but she'd made the most of the space: there were pots teeming with flowers on the patio, beautiful clematises climbing up the side of the wall and dahlias spread open in bright, pink bloom; they'd only just begun to flower. Tabby's favourites, though, were the almost-black cornflowers, a shock of vivid blue every few flower heads catching her eye. Gran had sent her a packet a few years ago, which she'd grown back home in Cheltenham. Then, they'd reminded her of Gran; now, they reminded her of home, so many miles away, being packed up. Soon, she'd have a new home here to think about.

She opened the comment box and took a deep breath in. *They weren't your favourite girls before*, she typed, but deleted it a second later.

'Tabby?' Gran's voice floated through the back door. 'Are you coming in for lunch?'

'Just a minute!' she called back, slipping her phone in her pocket and picking up her book.

Gran stood at the kitchen counter, cutting the crusts off a slice of bread. *She refuses to acknowledge I'm old enough to eat my crusts.*

'What were you doing out there, love? I thought the point of being outside was that you actually spent time doing something other than being glued to that mobile of yours.'

'Nothing really,' Tabby said. Her phone burned in her pocket.

'Well, don't spend too much time on it,' Gran said, wrapping her arm around Tabby's shoulders. 'I don't want you beating my high score on Candy Crush, do I?'

The surface of the kitchen table was covered with old TV magazines, bits of paper and empty medication boxes. Gran kept promising she'd tidy them up, but so far hadn't attempted it; one of these days, Tabby was going to take matters into her own hands. For now, though, she pushed everything to one side to make room and sat down.

'What have you got planned for the rest of the day?' Gran asked, joining her.

'Not much.' Tabby patted her book. 'Finishing this, I guess.'

And stalking Jess's Instagram.

'You could go out for a run. I see you brought your trainers with you. Why not pop out for a bit?'

'No, I really just want to get on with reading.' *I don't run. Not any more.*

'You didn't bring many books with you. I thought you'd have come with half your bookshelf in your suitcase!'

'What's with all the questions, Gran? There wasn't enough room to bring them all, and Dad made me clear loads out anyway. Apparently, I could have taken up an entire removal van with my bookshelf.'

'Well, you'll have to go to the library then. You brought your library card, didn't you?'

'I really am fine. Honestly.'

Tabby hated to get snappy, but she was content staying here, inside her blissful cocoon for ever, where the only irritation she had was Gran waking her up with One Direction blaring from her (old-school) CD player every morning. ('You do know they've been split up for years, right?' Tabby had asked, and received a sharp reply that yes, Gran did in fact know and it would be nice if Tabby never, ever mentioned 'Wayne' leaving because she was still highly emotional about it. Tabby hadn't bothered to correct her.)

Gran gave her a pointed look. 'It's either go to the library tomorrow or come to Zumba with me. Your choice! But if it's Zumba, I expect you to put the maximum amount of effort in. I saw you slacking last time. Rose and I could run rings around you and we have a combined age of a hundred and fifty-five.'

'All right, I'll go to the library. I'll leave you and Rose to OAP Zumba.'

Gran got up and placed her hands over Tabby's shoulders. 'If you change your mind, I've got some spare Lycra you can borrow. Hot pink, I think it is – perfect for your complexion!'

Tabby swatted her away, and their laughter mingled around them as Gran kicked her leg up in the air in an imitation of a Zumba move.

'You'll dislocate your new hips if you're not careful!'

'I'm invincible,' Gran replied. 'Don't you worry about me!'

Tabby felt the vibration of her phone inside her pocket.

Jess: So youve decided to run away early? Good luck with
that

Jess: You may be able to leave but youll never get away
from the fact that youre a complete loser

'Got a secret admirer?' Gran asked.

'No.' Tabby laughed it off. 'It's just one of those adverts asking me if I want a super summer saving on my phone bill.'

Palms sweating, Tabby put the phone back on the table; it clanked down harder than she'd intended. 'What would you say to a cup of tea?' *I've perfected the art of distraction.*

'I'd say you were the best granddaughter in the whole world.'

I don't know about that.

Coming soon! A brand-new summer romance
from the author of LOVE, SECRET SANTA!

Five festivals... one unforgettable Summer

LOVE
ON THE
MainStage

S. A.
DOMINGO